D0451582

THE ABYSS OF HUMAN ILLUSION

A NOVEL

Gilbert Sorrentino

WITH A PREFACE
BY CHRISTOPHER SORRENTINO

COFFEE HOUSE PRESS
MINNEAPOLIS
2009

COPYRIGHT © 2009 by the Estate of Gilbert Sorrentino
COVER AND BOOK DESIGN by Linda Strand Koutsky
AUTHOR PHOTOGRAPH © Vivian Ortiz

COFFEE HOUSE PRESS books are available to the trade through our primary distributor, Consortium Book Sales & Distribution, www.cbsd.com or (800) 283-3572. For personal orders, catalogs, or other information, write to: info@coffeehousepress.org.
Coffee House Press is a nonprofit literary publishing house. Support from private foundations, corporate giving programs, government programs, and generous individuals helps make the publication of our books possible. We gratefully acknowledge their support in detail in the back of this book.

To you and our many readers around the world, we send our thanks for your continuing support.

LIBRARY OF CONGRESS CIP INFORMATION
Sorrentino, Gilbert.
The abyss of human illusion / Gilbert Sorrentino.
p. cm.
ISBN 978-1-56689-233-9 (alk. paper)
1. City and town life—New York (State)—New York—Fiction.
2. Neighborhood—New York (State)—New York—Fiction.
3. Brooklyn (New York, N.Y.)—Fiction.
1. Title.
PS3569.O7A74 2010
813'.54—DC22
2009028064
3   5   7   9   8   6   4   2

PRINTED IN THE UNITED STATES

Sections of this book previously appeared in
Golden Handcuffs Review and *The Brooklyn Rail*.

THE ABYSS OF HUMAN ILLUSION

CONTENTS

A Note to the Reader

The Abyss of Human Illusion was begun by my father in
October 2003, and a first draft was mostly complete when he
was diagnosed with cancer in the fall of 2005. Both the disease
and its treatment rapidly incapacitated him, and he had little
physical or intellectual energy available to sit at his desk and
work. Despite this, he did work throughout his final months
to complete what he referred to matter-of-factly as "my last
book," finishing it a few weeks before his death in May 2006.
At the time, he provided me with a typescript, heavily corrected and with marginal notations, consisting of the main
sections of the novel, as well as a composition notebook in
which he'd drafted in longhand the brief glosses on these sections, which together comprise the book in its entirety.

In preparing the manuscript for publication, I encountered
one immediate problem. As his strength faded, my father's hand-
writing (somewhat difficult to read under the best of circum-
stances) deteriorated to the point of near illegibility. Determining

his intentions was made more difficult by his habitually precise, but not necessarily consistent or orthodox, approach to punctuation, typography, and so forth—the minutiae most commonly in question. Less frequently, although more problematically, I came across indecipherable words and phrases. Often these became clear in context, or were repeated elsewhere more legibly, and thus were easily transcribed. In some instances, though, I have taken an educated guess, drawing on my familiarity with my father's work and verbal mannerisms. I found these to be relatively simple decisions, although doubtless there are some presumptuous flaws in my leaps of conjecture.

My father never made the switch to word processing, and habitually made handwritten revisions and alterations to his work only periodically and at discrete stages in the process— the now-common practice, familiar to writers of my generation, of intermittent, even fitful, revision and the subsequently frequent creation of wholly updated "documents" was unknown to him. In other words, I was working with what amounted to a corrected first draft, and in places the absence of the author from several stages of composition could be felt. While some sections called for only minor modifications— the correction of obvious errors and unintentional inconsistencies, for example—others raised the issue of their suitability for inclusion. In the end, I decided to ready the manuscript in its entirety for publication, for reasons that readers, and certainly writers, may find interesting.

For much of his career, my father delighted in writing within formal constraints (a practice that gave rise to what may be his defining remark, "Form not only determines content, but form invents content."). Some of the forms he devised allowed tremendous opportunity for play, in other cases the approach demanded a rigorous observance of prescribed rules and procedures. Correspondingly, while sometimes the formal conceits in his novels are obvious or easily grasped (the algorithmic mechanism of *Aberration of Starlight;* the use of the Tarot deck in *Crystal Vision),* many of his later books offer a less apparent and/or more indeterminate structure, and it is among this latter group that *The Abyss of Human Illusion* belongs. Though one aspect of its structure is evident even from a cursory look at the book (Its fifty sections grow incrementally longer; while the first is around 130 words, the last is around 1,300), its other formal ambitions remain unclear (to me).

Add to this the fact that, as is often the case with my father's work, there is a dense measure of intertextuality present in the book—sections of the book refer, or seem to refer, to one another, to my father's other books, to episodes depicted in those other books, and to stories and poems by others (Section XVI, for instance, is a loose reinterpretation of Rimbaud's early poem, "Winter Dream."). Perhaps not-so-paradoxically, the technical goals my father set only rarely trumped his belief—his faith, even—in serendipity, accident, in the aesthetically justified deviation from constraint that the OuLiPo named the *clinamen;* in standing back and seeing for himself whether a thing was finished to his satisfaction. Ultimately, the correct artistic balance was something my father determined not by having fully executed a schematic requirement, but, for better or worse, in the scale of his hand.

Accordingly, while I have made surgical excisions and interpolative changes as described above, and while I have, on occasion, cut sentences, phrases, and even paragraphs where it seemed to me that my father abruptly galloped off on one of the well-lathered hobbyhorses he rode over the years, or bore down on something more heavily than I believed his finely calibrated sense of irony and sarcasm would have allowed to stand, I have gone no further in "editing" this book. The scale of my own hand, though competent and discerning, is not that of his, and that alone is enough to stop me. Perhaps in time, when Sorrentino scholarship is not the exclusive pursuit of devoted sons and other deviants, a definitive edition of *The Abyss of Human Illusion* will appear, and I can only hope that the patient soul who labors over it will find my judgments essentially sound.

None of this is intended to suggest that this is an unfinished volume, intended only for scholars and completists. My father, who never had a problem burying work that dissatisfied him, made quite clear his intention and desire that this book be published. And it should be noted that, despite his absence from his customary role in its preparation, it is, in the end, a book to which he literally brought the fullest measure of his energy and ability.

—Christopher Sorrentino

He sat and stared at the sea, which appeared all
surface and twinkle, far shallower than the spirit
of man. It was the abyss of human illusion that
was the real, the tideless deep.

—HENRY JAMES

— I —

Mundane things, pitiful in their mundane assertiveness, their sad isolation. Kraft French dressing, glowing weirdly orange through its glass bottle, a green glass bowl of green salad, a bottle of Worcestershire sauce, its paper wrapper still on. All are in repose, in their absolute thingness, under the overhead alarming bright light of the kitchen. They may or they should, they must, really, reveal the meaning of this silent room, this silent house, save that they won't. There is no meaning. These things will evoke nothing.

In years to come, almost three-quarters of a century, they still evoke nothing. Orange, green, incandescent glare. Silence and loss. Nothing. There might be a boy of four at the table. He is sitting very straight and is possibly waiting for someone.

"Who knows what evil lurks in the hearts of men?," the Shadow asks, and answers himself, "The Shadow knows." The Shadow knows every-thing. "The weed of crime bears bitter fruit. Crime does not pay." The soft and eerie voice states these opinions as fact. As truth. As the law. Then the Shadow begins to laugh, a terrible, monstrous, haunting laugh, and then steps softly out of the Philco floor-model radio, amazingly and terrifyingly out of the little orange-glowing arc of the dial.

He stands in his black cloak and black slouch hat, his face covered save for his vengeful, burning, hellish-black eyes. The boy turns pale and his heart stops beating for a moment. "The Shadow knows," the phantom says, and begins, again, merci-lessly, his unearthly laughter, laughter that his dead grand-mother would laugh, were she able.

— III —

H e had blundered through his life. He often thought of all the people he had known: those he had touched briefly, those he had loved or hated, those whose names or faces he clearly remembered, their voices. He considered how these people had not managed to ease or simplify his life, his way through life, perhaps, was the more accurate phrase, save for a moment here or there. But what had he expected, what had he wanted? It was, he knew, certain, that had he not known, in any way, all the people he had known, but had, instead, known as many wholly different people, his life, such as it was, would have been the same in its vast panoply of error and carelessness. He had indeed blundered through his life, as he would have blundered through any life given him. Had he been born anywhere at all—he *knows* this—he'd still be standing at a dark window, alone, wondering who, through the years, precisely he was. "Or who I am." It was going to snow again.

— IV —

Three windows look out on a cold, sunless street. A toy metal zeppelin, silvery in color, with a rigid vertical fin, rests on the floor on two bright red wheels. There are people in the room, there is laughter and conversation, a Christmas tree in the corner, situated so as to be seen from the street, projects its insistent multicolored lights into the room. A two-year-old boy sits on the zeppelin so as to ride it, to push it with his feet across the floor to where his mother sits with a highball, talking to another woman. The boy slides backwards on the zeppelin and feels a sharp pain as his buttocks strike the sharp fin. Blood seeps through his short pants and he begins to cry, holding his hands against the hurt. The blood runs down the boy's legs and into his socks.

His father jumps up from his place on the couch where he has been talking, quarreling, really, with his father-in-law, his highball spilling on his trousers. He steps toward the boy, his arms thrust out. His face is white.

— V —

The party was in a very dark apartment. It wasn't much of a party. There might have been twenty people there, or many more. There was a drone of what seemed to be conversation. There seemed too a drone of music coming from the walls. Sam was looking for his wife. She had gone into a little room off the living room with some people whom she apparently knew. Sam didn't know them. He knew one of them. He left the apartment and went down the stairs to the ground floor. His wife was at *that* party, he remembered. In the kitchen. He knew her friends. Or one of them. The door to the apartment was open. The apartment was just as dark as the other one. He went upstairs and got his coat. The cab was waiting right in front of the building. Somebody called down the stairs to say that it was only Saturday. His wife was sitting in a leather armchair. She was smoking a cigarette. Her coat was across her lap. He knew she wanted to leave. This woman was not his wife. She didn't look like his wife. She was wearing his wife's clothes. There were six people sitting on the floor in front of the woman. Their backs were to her. They looked at him with amusement. His wife began to emit a low drone. She wasn't his wife but he knew she was.

— VI —

ost of his friends were dead or far away, staggering into the apathy and complaint of old age. He
was, that is, virtually alone, his wife dead for
many years, his children distantly attentive, for-
mally so, but no more than that. When he
thought of his youth he could scarcely believe that his memories had anything at all to do with the absurd life he was
now living, an observation, he knew, that was far from original. Somehow, he had thought that *his* old age would miraculously produce finer, subtler notions of—what?—life? But
he was no better, no cleverer, no more insightful than any
shuffling old bastard in the street, absurdly bundled against
the slightest breeze.

He didn't know, or knew but refused to believe, that the
celebrations and joys, the razzmatazz, so to speak, of his youth
and young manhood, were perhaps perversely, yet precisely,
what had brought him to this disquiet, this discomfort, this

hidden and unacknowledged longing for oblivion. Had his youth been another sort of youth. . . . But it had not been, it had been his and his alone, and its clichés and blunders had led, almost sweetly, to the clichés and blunders of his senescence. Time to go and leave the world to the young, happily wallowing in the mess he'd left as a small part of their general inheritance.

— VII —

T he girls are on the beach at about three o'clock on a
sunny but cool July afternoon. Carol and Marsha and
Sheila. Berta and Minna, Nina and Ellie, Bea and
Diana and Natalie, Sydelle, Gloria, Margie, Marianne,
and Lona. They are all, this summer, in love, first love.
They look wonderful, they look pretty; they're beautiful.
Young and bronze and almost perfect in their absolute lack
of experience, their innocence that they think of as secret,
unique knowledge. They think that they have lived, but life
is waiting for them just beyond the beach, just past this particular summer, life with its loss and disillusion and tears, its
disease and pain and death. They are beautiful and fading
into oblivion.

He stands in the shade of a birch tree on the little island
separated from the beach by a shallow and fast-moving rill of
water, and he looks at the girls in their varied glamour: he *sees*
them. He sees, too, the girl with whom he is in love in this

disappearing summer, and who is in love with him. He will not say her name; he has his reasons, demented though they may be: he has his reasons. She, of course, is the most beautiful of all the girls and will always be so, he mistakenly thinks.

— VIII —

H
e gets up at 6:00 every morning and turns on the radio, so that he can listen to the news, concerning which, he cares nothing. He makes instant coffee and toasts a store-brand English muffin, which he slathers with peanut butter, eats and then lights a cigarette, one of the five or six he smokes every day, despite his doctor's warnings about the early signs of emphysema. After he clears the table and washes his few dishes, he goes into the living room, sits in his easy chair, and waits. He waits for news that the world will be ending by noon, that the president has fallen off a horse and broken his neck, that the mighty of the earth have all been vaporized. He waits to hear that Jesus has returned and has been married in Las Vegas. He waits, the radio blathering and droning, on and on.

His wife is dead, his children estranged, all his friends dead, too, or dying, or living in grim sunny places without sidewalks far away. Far away from what? he sometimes laughs, remembering the old story of the death camp survivor. He waits for everything to what? To get tired, to disappear, waits for all the filth to disappear, every mean fucking cold-eyed bastard to disappear, to be obliterated along with their victims, along with the dogs and cats and whales and showgirls, along with all the mothers and sisters and priests, along with all the money, the computers, the radios and the television sets, the news, the news, the news. BOOM.

— IX —

ach day, he'd sit at the kitchen table looking out the sliding glass door at the little patio that he had slowly grown to hate, he had no idea why. He'd sit and drink coffee and smoke and wait for the phone to ring with someone, anyone on the line to give him some news, good or bad or meaningless, it didn't matter. But the phone rarely rang, and when it did, it presented a message so empty, so anonymous, that it was merely a form of quiet noise.

Many years earlier, he'd had a friend, much younger than he, who had, "out of the blue," as they say, committed suicide. This friend had once told him that when he opened the paper each morning he would do so in the absurd yet overwhelming hope—perhaps even belief—that he'd come across a story in which he would figure as somebody, as anybody at all, as a name in the newspaper. He wanted, he said, to read some surprising news about himself: before he disappeared like all the other ciphers.

He looked out the window at the rain-washed patio and thought that he couldn't recall his young friend's name, nor, for that matter, his face. Then he realized that he'd been, perhaps, remembering another young man altogether, a character in a play or movie. A novel. Someone who had never been.

— X —

He loves a girl, who, as it turns out, does not love him, and so he wastes years of his life trapped in a wretched cliché. This is, as everyone knows, the oldest of news. At the time that he met the unattainable girl, another girl, whom he treated with a distant, friendly formality, tinged with a benign contempt, adored him and would have done anything for him, had he but asked. She was, as they say, "the girl for him." This is but more old news.

But since life is, essentially, and maddeningly, a series of mistakes, bad choices, various stupidities, accidents, and unbelievable coincidences, everything played itself out just as it should have; although a shift this way or that in this young man's life, an evening at a friend's house avoided, a day at the beach cut short because of rain—anything you can dream up, the more absurd the better—would have led to wholly different results, each one of which would have played itself out precisely the way it should have. There is no way to bargain with life, for life's meaning is, simply, itself. Perhaps this is why one society after another relentlessly invents its gods and the byzantine complexities of the religions in which those gods are enclosed forever: somebody to talk to, to cajole, to beg and bribe. That nothing helps doesn't matter, for, most importantly, the gods can be blamed. They "work in mysterious ways."

— XI —

Here is a bed in a room that glows in early morning light. The new white shades drawn against the sun soften the light to a pale yellow. A woman of perhaps twenty-five sits against the headboard, leaning back against two pillows, laughing. She has on a white nightgown, the bosom of ecru lace; the right shoulder strap has slipped down to her upper arm. Drawn to her waist is a pale-blue blanket and white counterpane.

A man sits on the edge of the bed, at its foot, wearing a white athletic shirt, and blue-and-white-striped boxer shorts. He, too, is laughing, half-turned toward the woman. The bed may be broken in some way, for it tilts at an angle to the floor. The man is a little younger than the woman, but beginning to lose his hair. He reaches toward her and touches her arm softly. She puts her left hand over his, and, just at that moment, the Angelus is heard faintly but clearly on the Sunday morning air.

A boy of three enters the room, and stands, happily looking at the enormous strangers on the bed. He is in Dr. Denton
pajamas, of a color almost identical to that of the blanket. The
light in the room is a little yellower. It's going to be a nice day,
but not a portent of days to come.

— XII —

hile he was at work each day, an old friend who was staying with him and his wife until he could find an apartment, and who was, in the meantime, perfectly at home in his hosts' apartment, passed the long days by making love to his friend's wife, whom he didn't much care for, but, well, there she was, vapid and bored and available.

The host felt, rather than knew, that the pair couldn't wait for him to leave for work in the morning so that they could happily get to their rutting. On weekends, the tension in the apartment virtually sizzled. The man had no knowledge, no proof, no evidence of his cuckolding, no hint was ever given, no suggestion, leer, no shifting of eyes.

Every day after lunch, the husband threw up, and every night, he would stare out the kitchen window for hours, smoking one cigarette after another. His friend found another apartment after three months and moved out, taking the husband's

Zippo lighter, a gold graduation-gift fountain pen, a can opener, all the change that was in a little bowl on the kitchen table, as well as three shirts, nicely selecting those fresh from the Chinese laundry.

His wife remarked, that first night, with an almost brilliant sincerity, that it was really good to have the place to themselves again. She was, of course, pregnant.

— XIII —

His doctor, surprisingly, not his dentist, is doing something profoundly invasive in his mouth. She's sliced open his gum, and is scraping and ripping and picking, with a sharp metal instrument, at tooth and bone. He doesn't feel any pain, but a remote, muffled discomfort, and a dull, insistent pressure has taken over his right eye and temple.

He realizes that he has, quite helplessly and without volition, gently closed his jaw on her fingers, and she tells him so, but his attempts to open his mouth are unsuccessful. She looks at him and smiles, but the smile is one of patronization, of domination, the same smile that she wears when he lies on her examination table and she palpates and fingers his abdomen, scrotum, and penis for signs of disease or possible malignancy. His concern, at these times, is that he will get an erection and embarrass himself and her.

He looks up at her smile and nods his head, then opens his mouth. Blood slides down his numb chin and onto the paper bib he wears over a plastic apron. She nods in turn and removes her skirt, then recommences her attack on the infection in his gum, her lower abdomen and thighs pressed against his shoulder. Perhaps she will mount him, carefully and silently, when she finishes the procedure. He hopes so, for he is thoroughly aroused.

— XIV —

hen his wife of thirty-four years died, he married, soon after, a beautiful aspiring actress who was, in the best tradition of the deathless cliché, half his age. He had met her five years earlier at a party in West Hollywood at a time when there had been "a lot of interest" in filming one of his books on which an option had been taken by an "edgy young producer." The "project" had, of course, come to nothing. The young actress grew bored with the marriage, discovering, after a year or so, that writers are, by and large, even more boring than their books; and so she left him to go back to Hollywood, where she worked in a few cinematic grotesqueries, occasional episodes of divers TV series, and a commercial or two: she made a living.

He is now almost seventy, and shows no signs of illness, lethargy, decrepitude, or depression. He turns out a novel every other year, and while they are no better than his earlier books, they are certainly no worse. Since he was famous for a charmingly mediocre novel published at the age of twenty-eight, he is still famous for his charming mediocrities, all of which serve to recall his first, to the delight of reviewers. And so honors and awards come to him at the rate of one a year. His is a life often held up to young students of "creative writing" by their "widely published" instructors, as the sort of life to which it behooves them to aspire, a life that wearily smiles, so to speak, at the notion of art, which it pronounces "art." He is, so it is said, on the short list for the Nobel Prize, and who is more deserving?

GILBERT SORRENTINO · 24

— XV —

The man was sexually and emotionally attracted to young mothers and had spent his adult life pursuing and, when he could, seducing them; he'd left a lot of wreckage behind. He met a woman, the mother of two boys, seven and five, a woman who was the wife of a casual friend. They "ran off together," as they used to say, leaving the two boys with their father, who was, not surprisingly, angry, bewildered, and, for the moment, heartbroken. The new couple soon had a child of their own, but the fact that the young woman was now the mother of her seducer's child ruined everything for him, and he left one day in their old Ford station wagon, a sun-faded lime-green monster that might well have served as a sad counter for their dead amour.

He took $147.34, all the money that was in the coffee can in the refrigerator of the wretched St. Louis apartment in which they lived, all the money that they had. Nobody who had known them in New York ever discovered why they had moved to St. Louis, and when the young woman returned, bitter and humiliated, to her husband and two older children, she never told them, except for some vague references to "teaching jobs." Her husband, perhaps understandably, treated the new child as if he were a demanding visitor who would soon miraculously disappear. As for his wife, he thought of her as a stupid maid whom he occasionally and quite gently, he thought, raped.

— XVI —

n the winter of that year, after his post basic training leave, he took a train to San Antonio, to report for duty at Fort Sam Houston; he would be there for three months, at the Medical Field Service School, for advanced training. On the train, he discovered that the club car was painted a pale rose; its armchairs were a soft feathery blue. A girl came in and he and she began to talk. It was very late and they were alone in the car and quite comfortable together. The train drove through the darkness, and the promise of kisses lay in every dim corner.

After a time, the girl closed her eyes to the night rushing by outside the windows, the silent night in which black demons and black wolves ran silently through the black countryside. The train crashed on through the darkness.

He leaned toward her and kissed her cheek, then her ear, then put his lips in a light spidery touch on her neck, first at her hairline, then down to the collar of her dress. How sweet she smelled.

"It feels like a spider," she said, "so soft and light. You'd better catch it." He took a long time finding that spider; for the little monster roamed everywhere under her clothes, everywhere.

The next morning, at sunrise, the train pulled into Dallas and she got off. He waved to her from his coach window, but she pretended not to see him. The sky was turning rose and blue.

He wasn't intrinsically contemptible, yet there was no way, it seemed, that he could avoid being thought of with contempt, at least not by those who got to know him, men and women alike. There was a sweetness about him, an attractive innocence, when he forgot what he thought he was supposed to be; what, it sometimes appeared, he had been mysteriously instructed to be. But these instances of candor were few and short-lived.

Most of the time he was at his worst, and this worst always manifested itself in the same way: he flagrantly and openly and with a kind of nauseating pride—real or constructed— insisted on boasting of his flaws and faults as if they were virtues.

To note a pedestrian example of his irritating pretensions: he rarely combed or brushed his hair and, even more rarely, shampooed it; so that it was a greasy, matted tangle that smelled of rancid and sour fat. This aberration, which he would, of course, call attention to, would too, without fail, prompt him to remark that this was the way of Greek warriors, the way that Odysseus and Achilles dressed their hair. He used the word, "dressed." It was this sort of thing, this sort of foolish affectation that made him an object of contempt, sometimes seasoned with a vague pity.

When he died, rather suddenly, of a heart attack, nobody really cared, although there were the usual insincere obsequies. But someone said, in a fair imitation of his voice, "Death is a *groove*, man!"

— XVIII —

She was an old woman now, as he was an old man, and seeing her made him realize just *how* old he really, as they say, was. He thought of her as she looked, God, *forty-five* years ago?, as she looked on the night that he and she had surrendered to their desire for each other, a surrender nicely camouflaged by and blamed on their having had "too much to drink." But he knew the truth and so did she. From that moment on, he relegated their lapse to the simplest of reasons, lust and its gratification, and that was, as they say, that. She soon married a friend of his and had two children, and he remained, surprising himself, a bachelor.

They sat in the booth of the diner in the old neighborhood, a renovated and renamed diner, but the same old place, and talked over coffee. They had just come back from the cemetery where she'd buried her husband and were on the way to her elder daughter's house where the mourners would be fed, in time-honored fashion. He had suggested coffee first and here they were.

She seemed smaller than ever, her face thin and lined, her hair gray with a subtle wash of old-lady pale blue in it. Her breasts were virtually nonexistent, but her legs were still good, especially in the sheer black stockings she'd worn for the funeral. So you're what, he said, sixty what? You know how old I am, she said, sixty-eight, eight years younger than you. You know that and you've always known that. That's right, he said. Eight years. So we were twenty-three and thirty-one, he said. What do you mean? she said, When? Oh. Right, he said. You've been thinking of *that* all these years? she said, laughing. Not *all* the time, he said, Jesus! He put on an amused face, but he was blushing, and realized that he probably looked like a complete idiot. But once in a while, he said, and thought: more than you know. He felt absolutely, sickeningly empty.

— XIX —

$\int$ he is standing at the sink in a gloomy kitchen, the pale-
gray light from the sole window its only illumination.
She's wearing white rayon underpants and a matching
brassiere, white cotton socks and slippers whose fluffy,
artificial blue fur has been worn to the nap. She's wash-
ing her lunch dishes—a sandwich plate, a cup and saucer, and
a table knife. She looks up and to her right, for she feels as if
someone is looking at her.

The window looks out on a gray courtyard, its concrete dark-
ening with beginning rain. She stands on her toes and looks out
into the courtyard, for she feels that someone, certainly, is looking at her. She puts the saucer on the drainboard, and dries her
hands, then folds her arms protectively across her breasts, and
looks with what might be longing at her bathrobe, draped over
the back of a kitchen chair, wanting to snatch the robe up and
put it on now, quickly, before something happens. She finds it
impossible to move, to take the step toward the chair.

She leans against the sink, her thighs clamped together, and looks at the kitchen doorway, into the living room. Her body is rigid and she is flushed. Someone is looking at her from the courtyard or the living room. She looks at her robe again, and almost takes a step toward the kitchen chair, but does not. She is a week or so into her thirty-ninth year, and knows that she is not bad-looking, and knows that men do look at her, they do. Someone is looking at her now. She knows that this is really not so.

She puts on her robe, wishing, perhaps, that someone would look at her, that someone in the courtyard, in the living room, some nameless phantom were waiting for her, someone to whom she could abandon herself, some beast, some animal, some sex fiend, for whom she could throw herself away, for whom she could recklessly damn herself to pleasure and hell.

— XX —

He died in a monstrous blooming rose of blood and fire outside of Munsan-ni, under a mortar attack. A week earlier, Chinese rounds had tracked a squad across a valley floor with relentless, elegant, fussy precision, killing two and wounding two.

Before his orders had been cut for Fort Ord and FECOM, he was stationed for a brief time at Fort Meade, Maryland. A friend of his, in the Marines at Camp Lejeune, thought it might be a good idea if they met maybe in Baltimore for a weekend of disorderly drunkenness, etc. He said O.K., and they agreed to meet at a bar on Charles Street that they both knew. He got out to the highway on a post bus to hitchhike, in clean and starched Class-A khakis. What a soldier, standing tall!

After ten minutes, a powder-blue Cadillac Coupe deVille rocketed to a halt just past him, and then backed up, whitewalls screaming, and he got in. The driver was going to

Wilmington, and he'd take him right into fuckin' Baltimore. He was a man of maybe fifty, sunburned and sweaty and absolutely drunk in that placid way that alcoholics know how to polish to perfection. On the seat, between his legs, was a quart of Gordon's gin, from which he drank regularly. He'd occasionally light a Pall Mall, at which times he'd steer with one knee, smiling childishly. He maintained an average speed of about eighty-five to ninety miles an hour, looking at the road, or so it seemed, but now and again. At one point, the car hit a patch of gravelly sand and sailed through the summer air, quite beautifully, for some twenty yards, while the driver hooted with pleasure at, perhaps, the sight of death, grinning on the hood. But the Caddy landed gently and on they went, spared for something or other. We know why the soldier was spared, of course.

Incidentally, the driver offered the soldier a drink and a cigarette only after their unexpected flight: maybe he thought they were now true comrades.

— XXI —

t became clear to Larry and Martha that she didn't, much of the time, really hear what he said to her, even though she responded in what he had thought, for some years, to be a cogent and rational way, if sometimes tangentially or abstractly. Martha absorbed Larry's words, in some curious way, their rhythms, grammatical structures, and syntagmatic relationships, but the content of these words—assuming that there was, on occasion, "useful" content—were, to Martha, empty of meaning or even allusions to cognate meanings. She made courageous stabs at what he said, tried hard to *listen*, but her guesses—for that's what they came to—were, unsurprisingly, most often startlingly wrong. So Martha constructed for their marriage an improvisatory fantasia: what Larry *said* became what Larry did not say, which, in turn, became what he really said—the latter Martha's total invention. So their domestic intercourse proceeded, a strange path discoverable only as it was traveled.

That Larry came to accept and then believe that what he had not said was what he had *said*, and that the converse was also the case, is perhaps, surprising, but only if it is not known that Larry never remembered just what he *had* said. He was easily convinced that opinions that he did not hold were dear beliefs, and so on. As words left his mouth, they disappeared into oblivion, or, in this case, into Martha's linguistic workshop. So their marriage moved along, a series of deft disguises, masquerades, and incredible stories, a kind of anthology of make-believe. Both of them came to embrace the world that their conversations created as if it was life itself—it was, in a way, of course, and no worse, really, than that loved by couples who pride themselves on the honesty and candor that most often leads to misery. Their marriage was, as Larry would put it, "swell," which Martha would call "deeply respectful of each other's feelings."

— XXII —

t was a little vanity case, its cloth covering worn and faded with years and use. It had also been subjected to the moisture of the various bathrooms in which she'd kept it since well before they were married. It sported a small, blurred, essentially useless mirror on the inside of its lid, and in its compartments were lipsticks, tweezers, nail files, emery boards, mascara, cuticle scissors, and the like.

On its outer lid there was an inept cartoonish drawing of a little girl in pigtails and a tulip-patterned dress, and a little boy in shorts, holding hands. They wore imbecilic and oddly sinister smiles. Above these figures, in a semicircle, were the words, HANDLOME IL AL HANDLOME DOEL. He read these words every day over the seven years that they'd been married, and in his self-centeredness, and supreme lack of curiosity, he had assumed that this message was some soppy maxim, an insufferable platitude in a bastard language whose phonemes were strangely close to English yet repulsively distant and vulgar.

After he discovered that his wife had been relentlessly unfaithful to him with God knows how many men, friends, acquaintances, pickups, the butcher, the baker—anyone in pants, as they say—and often in their bed—"their" took on a grim comic shimmer in his mind—they separated. Some months later, in a kind of sudden dazzle of lucidity, he read, he understood, he *saw* clearly the message on the vanity case—of course! *Handsome is as handsome does.* Of course! He stepped back as if slapped, for the obscurity of the message lay, all those years, in its candor. The message was, this he knew, a counter, a sign for his wife, somehow. He did not know how to put this, or think about this, but the plain message, which to him was unreadable, was *her* message. She had always been in plain sight, but he had failed to see her, he had dismissed her, he had not read or cared to read that which had been, always, before him.

— XXIII —

The elevator is huge, the size of a small apartment, and is filled with rows of desks, more, it would appear, than can fit into the space. On the rear wall of the elevator is a blackboard with chemical and mathematical symbols scattered across its surface. The door opens and he is on the sixth floor of the building in which he lived just after his divorce. This was his floor and he walks down the corridor, its walls now filthy, smeared with dirt and grease, the tiles underfoot pitted, scarred, and broken. He comes to his door and checks the apartment number, which is, rather strangely, he thinks, 6&6$6%. But he opens the door.

The apartment is the one he lived in when he was a little boy, complete with the faded brown studio couch, the Philco floor-model radio, and the hammered copper bas-relief reproduction of *The Last Supper*, with its Latin inscription across the upper border: AMEN DICO VOBIS QUIA UNUS VERSTRUM ME TRADITURUS EST. He hears a noise in the kitchen and looks away from the vaguely glowing image on the wall to see his mother standing in the kitchen doorway.

She seems pleased to see him, even though he is clearly startled at her appearance, that of a young woman in a summer pinafore, her blond hair in a loose chignon. He is about to speak to her, when she says, "I hope you're not hungry, I'm dead." She is apologetic and he remembers that the reason he is here is to tell her why he wasn't with her when she died. He knows that he won't tell her the truth, but decides that a lie is all to the good in this situation, especially with the radio tuned to *The Make-Believe Ballroom*. She smiles at him and says that it's all right, she knows that he wanted to be there, and "after all, who wants to travel in the bitter cold to Jersey City?!" She sits on the studio couch and motions for him to sit next to her. "I thought I'd ask you over so that we can listen to the *Lux Radio Theater*," she says. "Lana Turner is on tonight. They discovered her in a drugstore, you know." The radio is playing Bix Beiderbecke's "Margie," and he starts to laugh.

— XXIV —

Vince didn't like people to do what he regularly accused them of never doing, if, that is, these people performed these acts after being told by Vince that they never thought to perform them. Perhaps he thought that the acts, performed precisely as he regularly complained that they were never performed, were somehow sullied or cheapened because of the fact that they occurred after his complaint. This may seem absurd to the point of a tattered neurosis, but such is the world. There are more serious insanities to ponder, surely, but we are, for the moment, caught in the toils of this one.

For instance, let's assume that Vince's wife, had he a wife, never brought home from the store a particular brand of cereal that Vince liked, and that Vince often mentioned this. If, on his wife's next shopping trip, she brought home the *favored cereal*, Vince would say, in irritation and contempt, tinged with sadness, that the only reason that she'd brought home the cereal was because he'd noted that she never brought it home. The cereal was diminished in value, likewise the act of buying it, because this act had not been his wife's idea, but his.

So Vince rather sullenly lived his life, slowly and steadily being deprived by others of many—oh, many—things that he desired (and not only tangible things, but words, acts, even let's say, emotions and "states of being"), since others simply stopped responding to his complaints of their neglect and blithe thoughtlessness. Why bother? may well have been their rationale. He never quite knew what ultimately hit him—and hit him and then hit him again. What he did know was that nobody, not a single person, honored his requests, his desires, his *needs,* before he was compelled to voice them, and when he did voice them they ignored him. They ignored him! It had not always been thus, but what it had been, indeed, was crass and crude, no better than the current situation, which revealed his friends, his imaginary wife, his colleagues at work, anyone who had the least acquaintance with him, to be shallow and selfish. How wonderful it was to be right.

— XXV —

n his old age, childless and thrice-divorced, with all of
his old friends either dead, sick, or gone to sunbaked
funereal places that were beyond his wish even to imagine them, Arthur began, one day, with no plan to speak
of, to tote up, idly, to be sure, his grievances: the slights
he'd endured, the insults, the petty humiliations unanswered
and unavenged. He listed the unreciprocated kindnesses he'd
shown others, the unanswered letters, the snubs, hurts, bad
manners revealed, the advantage taken of him by those he had
considered friends, or, at the least, not enemies. The project,
if it may be given such a name, overwhelmed him, and he
began to recover incidents, long forgotten, that he added,
painstakingly and precisely, to his cruel catalog. He felt as if
driven before a wholly unexpected avalanche.

He bought a notebook, rather, an accounting ledger, and
meticulously divided it into twenty-six sections, given over
alphabetically to those people he had, for the most part, fished

out of oblivion. Now he could enter, with great care, all that these people had, he knew, he remembered, done to him. After each name—sometimes, when he had forgotten the name that went with the now-despised face, he would simply describe the person in a mnemonic shorthand—he wrote a carefully constructed synopsis of the sneer, the slight, the shabby act or remark that he attached to the person so recalled. Unsurprisingly, perhaps, Arthur pulled out of the pit of lost years, miseries long buried, and these would serve to illuminate others, many others, in their various darknesses. And, too, many of the wounds he felt once again were, to put it gently, imagined wounds. But they were added to his expanding lists.

His book, after a year or so, begot another, and then yet another, as his grievances grew and flowered, so that this accounting became his entire occupation. He was, if the word may be given a perverse reading, supremely content. A shabby euphoria, a Calvinist paradise.

— XXVI —

He sat in a latticed-metal patio chair at a metal table so battered by time and weather that its stained, dirty-white enameled surface was pitted and gouged, thoroughly ravaged by large areas of rust. The sun was low in his eyes.

He was drinking canned 3.2 beer from a case that sat half under the table on the concrete floor; the beer was warm and metallic in his mouth and he'd drunk eighteen cans of it: he wasn't, however, really drunk. Surely, he could stand up easily and walk into the beer hall from which a low-pitched roar of aimless anger and boredom and hilarity issued without cease. The other tables on this little concrete apron were mostly empty, but here and there other drunks sat drinking resignedly.

He could easily, easily walk into the beer hall but he didn't care to, no. Above the low monotonous din there now floated a female singer's voice, all blond and clean, remarking on the fact that she is lonesome and sorry and wondering if you are too, whoever you is. Then she stopped but the roar went on. He pulled open his fly buttons and slid himself forward on the chair, then pissed on the concrete between his feet, while he drank, stupidly, from a fresh can of beer. Maybe the drunks at the other tables would notice the pool of urine spreading on the concrete beyond his table, but they didn't and they wouldn't. They're all pissing on the ground, too, he thought. He knew it. Nobody wanted to go to the latrines in the beer hall, for Christ's sake.

Somebody—two somebodies—came out onto the concrete apron, headed for an empty table, each carrying a case of beer: one had Lone Star, the other Pearl. They were smoking and laughing, squinting into the late sun in their shining new fatigues. It was Rosie! One of them was Rosie! And the other was Koenig? Koenig! It was amazing, it was amazing, amazing. He put both hands on the table to push himself up on his feet and walk through the little pond of his urine, Rosie would see how dumb and funny that was, he'd walk over and say hello to them, Rosie and Koenig. Sit down and remember that chickenshit motherfucker platoon sergeant who got killed, thank God, just like they got killed. But now they were back, back here in the grim Texas sunlight, back and alive among the drunken living. They didn't die after all? Only that cracker prick of a sergeant got it, checked the fuck *out*. Good. He got ready to get up, he could do it, easy.

— XXVII —

More stories than we care to acknowledge are poignant yet wholly banal, and perhaps those that we insist on as poignant are not that at all, but are, rather, bathetic, sentimental, saccharine, or, even more dreadful, creakingly "worldly." Perhaps this one fits the mold, if it can be called a story.

There were two friends, young men, filled with idealism, and the love, just burgeoning, for art and the artist's life. We know them well. One becomes a high school English teacher, the other moves to Los Angeles and begins work at a talent agency in Beverly Hills, in, of course, the mailroom. After a few years he opens his own agency, and ten years later, is successful and rich, a millionaire "many times over."

The friends' correspondence, once brisk and regular, slowly peters out into a letter now and again, strained and brief, and finally settles into the official "holiday greetings and how is Susan" cards. The teacher is sure—and in this he is correct—

that his millionaire friend stopped writing first because he has passed beyond their youthful friendship and become "too good" for him, although he does not think this prim and vaguely parental phrase. Here he is, in Queens, while "the famous agent"—and he *does* think *this*—shops on Rodeo Drive and has dinner with movie stars.

But the reason that the Los Angeles friend stopped writing is more subtle than this, more convoluted, perhaps. He broke off the correspondence because of his muddled belief that his old friend has long held him in contempt for his success, and for how that success was achieved; that he had somehow sold out his talents, his artistic soul, etc., etc. But this is not true, the teacher has always been pleased for if envious of his friend, and has, very unlike him, known, ever since they were just past their post-adolescence, that neither of them were artists, nor had any talent for art of any kind, and that his friend did not know this. He often recalls a letter that he received soon after his friend went to work for the agency, the gist of which was that it would be a great place to gather material for his novel, which he had finally *seriously* started. It was, of course, never ended.

This is, as suggested, not much of a story, although another writer, Henry James for an ideal instance, might be attracted to its small cruelties and faint ironies and take it on.

— XXVIII —

Steve had subscribed to the *New Yorker* for some seven or eight years, and doggedly read all the fiction in every issue, trying to absorb and internalize, I suppose is a just word, the strained sophistication of the prose, its nervous hipness, aloof disingenuousness, its remote, somewhat bored whimsy. It goes without saying, perhaps, that he had "submitted" his own stories, they were many, to the magazine for five years, faithfully sending a story out on the day after he got one back, its rejection slip clipped to his beautifully printed-out "stuff," as he called his work. There was never a note, encouraging or otherwise, written on the slips; for that matter, it was my fantasy that the rejection slips were attached to the papers in a strangely dissociated way, that they had somehow found the stories and seized upon them as prey: no human agency seemed ever to have been involved. I once suggested that he send his stories to a magazine that was, well, not as impressed with itself but he gave me, as it is said, a *look*.

I sometimes wanted to tell him my own opinion of the magazine's fiction, but never did, for it is not possible to use the phrase "a *New Yorker* story," without its devotees hustling to the journal's defense, smirking at one's gauche ignorance, and telling—and telling again—the offending and pitiable ignoramus that there is no such *thing* as a *New Yorker* story, that there might have been, years ago, such a thing, but that now—look, just look!—Hip and Engaged and Transgressive and Absolutely Unexpected, brékékékék koáx koáx, and just plain *Well Written!* They wouldn't publish *Faulkner* for Christ's sake! Not their sort of thing.

So I said nothing; on the contrary, I took notes on certain stories, on certain phrases, on bright wise similes, so that Steve and I could discuss their subtleties. I don't know why I did this, save that I was feeling a little bad for him. One day, the latest issue had a story in it written by a young woman who had been, ten years earlier, in a writing workshop with Steve at the New School. Steve read the story three or four times that first day, turning to look at the author's name— Joye Lapidus—again and again, her name in that "beautiful, beautiful" *New Yorker* typeface. It is beautiful, I said, classic, traditional, aristocratic, really. Look at the "e" in "Joye." He nodded, and I knew he was seeing "Steven."

— XXIX —

he old man knew he was dying. The doctor had come after an episode of terrible agony that he'd endured that morning, and after the briefest of looks at his patient, who twitched and writhed and rocked in pain, he said that he wanted him admitted to the hospital immediately. But the stubborn old fool refused to go in an ambulance, and the doctor, who knew his catalog of neuroses and prejudices and insanities virtually by heart, said that he'd drive him in his car, which was parked right in front of the building. "I'll not have the horse's ass gawms staring at me in an ambulance, by Jesus," the old man said. "Goddamned fools and creeping Jesus Lutherans, may God damn them to hell."

He asked the doctor to go down and wait in his car, he'd be right down, he wanted to put on some clothes, he'd be goddamned if he'd leave the house in his pajamas like some shanty Irish greenhorn. The doctor told him not to be too long, then repeated this information accompanied by a pointing and admonishing index finger, and left.

The old man put on a starched white shirt, a dark-blue tie with a small light-blue paisley figure on its ground, an Oxford gray shadow-striped suit with vest, black shoes and black silk socks, and a gray homburg. Then he left, with his daughter, who had been standing, during the doctor's visit, in the kitchen, looking out at the neighboring roof. She didn't want to have this sick father, she didn't want to have this dead father, she didn't want to have to be alive to put up with this. But here she was; with this mean, dying old man. She was afraid and relieved that he'd probably not recover this time.

On the landing between the ground and second floor, the old man stopped, stood straight for a moment, then bent over and vomited black, grainy blood, once and then again. He wiped his mouth with his handkerchief, then inspected his shoes and trouser cuffs for stains. "You'd better clean this mess up, Skeezix," he said, "the Scowegian will have a fit and you'll never hear the end of it." She went back up the stairs. "I'll be at the hospital as soon as I get dressed," she said, and he waved her away and, panting with the pain in his innards, continued down, cold sweat making his face shine resplendently with doom.

When she'd cleaned up the vomit, she went upstairs again, dressed, left the building, walked to the nearby hack stand, and was at the hospital in twenty minutes, to discover that he'd died in the doctor's car. Later, back in the apartment, walking about in her slip, a private luxury that she suddenly became happily aware of, she found his watch and chain, his sterling silver pocketknife, and his wallet, with some four hundred dollars in it, on the dresser in his bedroom. She could hear his voice clear in her mind: "The hospital is nothing but a den of thieves. Worse than the goddamn firemen." She sat down on the bed and lit one of his Lucky Strikes. "Bye-bye, Poppa," she said.

— XXX —

He was certain that a man at his wife's office, a co-worker, of whom she spoke patronizingly but of whom she spoke every day, had become her lover. And when she joined a gym or an aerobics class or an exercise group or whatever it was that she joined, it was, surely, so that she could have a reason to be out of the house every Tuesday night for the obvious purpose.

He was delighted by this surprising, wholly unexpected occurrence, this astonishing "bump," as it were, in their marriage; but he did his best to feign his disappointment on Tuesday evenings, and even, sometimes, show a touch of irritation at not having her company—"not even for supper," as he would occasionally grumble. And, too, he would sometimes, in a small twitch of malice, ask her questions about her "nights out," sometimes causing her to lie so childishly that she would blush at her efforts. It was satisfying for him to watch, in a travesty of innocence, her discomfiture.

His marriage to her was an absurdity, but she was doing and had done as she'd promised before the wedding: she'd stay at her well-paid job and he'd stay at home to write. He had not yet been published, but had three "really encouraging" letters from important magazines, and he was actively looking for an agent, and he was working, more or less, on his first novel. She never complained and even took the garbage out and did all the grocery shopping on Saturdays or Sundays. When she began to commit adultery, he thought, just for a moment, as they say, that she, well, she *deserved* some fun. But what most enthralled him was the notion, the idea, the hope that she was in love with the office gallant and would, perhaps, leave home, but somehow continue to pay the bills. This was, no matter how it was sliced, an impossibility—if she left him, he'd be forced to go to work, and literature would be the poorer. He may have even thought something like this— surely, he had a fairly high opinion of his talents, else why, after all, would he write? Why indeed?

But, he thought, but perhaps he could persuade her to take a vacation now, that is, in the winter, get away from her job, her responsibilities, the apartment and the grind, baby, and, well, let's face it, *him*. If he did it right, hauled out his self-deprecating smile, if he didn't seem too anxious, he might get her to take two weeks, even three, and spend that time—as she would, wouldn't she?—with her lover down in the romantic Caribbean. She'd pay the bills up to date, of course, and leave him cash for food and incidentals. He'd be alone, taken care of, and free to hope that her admirer would beg her to come and live with him so that their idyll could become permanent. On the other hand, he might well grow tired of her, idyll or not, and sooner rather than later. This worried him, but in the meantime, there were Tuesdays.

— XXXI —

He didn't quite know what was happening to him, but something was happening to him, surely. Or had it happened already? Probably. Or had it been happening all along, as they say? Perhaps. It certainly was sharply reminiscent of what had happened to him— at least once—in the past. But what "past"? Yesterday? Two weeks ago? Nineteen forty-nine? Or longer ago than that? He was old enough to know that he'd forgotten many things that were once of urgent importance. What things? Had it happened in the days of Juicy Fruit and the Milano Restaurant, the latter long gone? And did they still make Juicy Fruit gum the same? What "sort" of thing had happened to him as he stood on the cold Manhattan street outside the Milano, his mouth packed with Juicy Fruit, his hand in his mother's hand; they were waiting for his father? They were waiting for his father. Is that all that happened? What did that have to do with what was happening to him now? And did *this* bring to mind the Milano? The cold streets, the pinkish wash of the sky over the Hudson River? Juicy Fruit? The Milano. The Milano. It had no significance for him, yet he remembered it, only as a name, though. Nothing more specific, save for the open boxes of cigars in the glass case by the cash register. His father bought a cigar and talked to the owner in Italian as he paid him. Is that what happened? Did he ever actually go to the Milano, or was the place existent only in his mother's stories? But he had had a mouth full of Juicy Fruit. Is he becoming a little hazy in his mind? He is. What is happening to him is happening to him, let it go at that. Whatever happened, then, happened during the Great Depression, of which his grandfather, years later, slightly drunk on cheap whiskey, liked to say, "what was so great about it?" *That* happened. Was it the war that had happened to him? The brave and necessary war, the war that "we" hated, but fought to end This and stop That and make sure that The Other Thing would never happen again, or at least not for four or five years. That must have been it. It? What *happened*, of course. That was *it*. If Hitler and Tojo and Mussolini and somebodies here and there—the Axis—had won, what then? If they had got the BOMB first, what then? They would have dropped it on—us? An unholy act. It *didn't* happen. If they had the planes and the tanks and the vast industrial might of a brave free people with lots of time and a half and double time on Sundays, what then? If *they* had been an Aroused Giant or two? Something else would be happening to him right now, and many other different things would have happened to him already. Death?

Is *that* what is happening to him? What are the telltale signs of death, anyway? One may be the well-dressed man who has quietly entered his room and who looks very much like Fredric March, who did a "brisk trade" back in the days of the Great Depression and the righteous war that brought it to a happy close. He is pleased that he remembers Fredric March, whom he always thought of, to be truthful, as a hambone.

— XXXII —

T he old man who lived in the apartment above his had a slight limp and wore a prosthetic shoe of some sort, black, ugly, and heavy, and such was the nature of his handicap, that it compelled him, it seemed, to wear the shoe all the time, so that he limped and clumped and shuffled about on his obviously rugless floors. In addition to this thumping, he played both his television and his radio at such a high volume that his neighbor could hear virtually every word spoken or screamed by the hysterical or ecstatic or soberly serious sports broadcasters and news anchors and reporters who were, apparently, the only representatives of the "news and entertainment world" permitted into the apartment of the relentlessly noisy old man.

Yet the neighbor never complained, for he had invented an entire if sketchy history for the old man, one which cast him in the role of the outcast and marginalized elder who had lost everything: whose wife had died in misery; whose children were callous and ungrateful; who had lost his friends to death and illness and dementia. He dressed badly, most often in baggy gray twill pants, faded and threadbare flannel shirts, ragged-edged suspenders, and scuffed and virtually colorless shoes, one of which, of course, was the weird monstrosity that apparently rarely came off his foot. He was certainly a veteran of the Second World War, wounded, but not gallantly, in action and now living precariously on his small disability payments and his equally small Social Security check. For what could he have been other than a clerk in some office in the financial district, some nervous nobody in a shiny black suit and not-too-fresh frayed shirt, carrying papers from one file drawer to the next for thirty years or more? He was a widower, yes, surely, a bit of detritus, flotsam, one of life's insulted; and so if he clumped and banged aimlessly about while listening to baseball or football or basketball or who the hell knew? bowling or billiards or marbles, that was but a minuscule recompense for the life he was living and had lived.

One afternoon, the sound of the television was so loud that the neighbor's apartment was brutally, almost, one might say, contemptuously assaulted, the noise a palpable entity in the air, the walls, the ceiling; the noise seemed to emerge from the drains in the sinks and bathtub, from the toilet bowl, it was cruel. He *had* to go upstairs and ask him to please, to please, to if you don't mind. So he went upstairs.

He knocked at the door and then rang the bell of this pathetic, probably half-deaf old man. He knocked again. The door opened and a woman of perhaps forty, not quite forty, lovely of face and figure, stood in the doorway. She was in a yellow raw-silk robe, partly open to reveal her near-nude body, one that the gossamer robe seemed rather to emphasize than conceal. Can I help you? she said, maybe. He didn't know what she said. She said something. The noise behind her was shattering, but she smiled at him, blithely, happily. Is there something that we can do? Or something. She said something. Her smile was friendly but slightly patronizing, the sort of smile that the young reserve for old men. She looked at him looking at her and pulled the robe closer around her body. Oh, he said. I thought, he said. But he did not say what he thought.

— XXXIII —

He is about halfway through the book of poetry, the selected poems of one of his friends, published some two months earlier, but only recently acquired. He turns a page and feels a touch, a nudge, a slight caress of nausea, and then, quickly, it overwhelms him, his stomach tumbles and writhes and cold sweat pops out on his brow and scalp. He puts the book on the desk, the pages flat on its surface. His shirt, he realizes, is soaked, and he gags, then rises to rush to the bathroom when he realizes that the nausea has passed. He sits down in his chair and leans back, looks out the window at his street crusted over with an inch or two of new snow, as he wishes he were.

He wishes, too, that he had a cigarette, that he'd never given up smoking, what was the point of it? He wishes this, he wishes that, he wishes his old bar hangout was still open, Christ oh Christ what doesn't he wish? He picks up the book and closes it, places it at the side of his desk, the book, this book by a friend of his, this book that has made his gorge rise, and he smiles at the worn-velvet cliché. "My gawje has rizzed," he says to the book. This is a book of some two hundred and fifty poems, by a friend of his, not a close friend but a friend nonetheless. And yet the poems have sickened him. He is on the edge of feeling shame: doesn't he like poetry? Did he ever like it? Is everything he's ever said or thought about it a lie, accompanied by a pose and a fake biography, pushed this way a little, turned that way a little more, and, overall, a shabby clutch of faded aesthetics. Maybe. Perhaps. It's too late to care.

More to the point, really, is the true cause of the nausea not the poems themselves but that they were written by his friend? That's what he should face: does he despise him? His friend is a great success in the small, almost always weaselly world of poetry, its sweaty ambitions, its minuscule rewards, its grim teaching appointments, its pathetic prizes, its insincere enthusiasms. His friend's career grew and blossomed by means of—of what? It is this carefully built career that the man won't look at, won't face. He picks up the book and riffles the pages. Oh for *Christ's* sake, think it, say it. By means of a determined transformation. His friend, an arrogant, selfish, cruel, egocentric yet charming man of sociopathic bent, to put the very best face on it, changed, oh yes, transformed his public presence into one of a subtly nuanced and delicate humility, transformed his entire life and world into the very picture of the sensitive artist, forever grateful and decently but not egregiously or embarrassingly humble before the attentions paid him, oh yes indeed. Thanks, thanks, thanks, he can hear him, thanks, so wonderful to be here, how kind of you all.

He sits in glum silence, thinking, knowing that the whole truth that he has admitted, if it is truth, is too tawdry to be sad, too banal to be bitter. Why, though, has it taken him so long to realize, to admit that his friend, his caring, concerned friend, warmly open to the earth and all the men and women on its roiling and corrupted surface, is not only a relentlessly self-promoting careerist, but worse, a third-rate poet? The fault is his, but he will not, he will never examine it.

— XXXIV —

They had decided to go on what Basil called an "excursion" into the mountains, such as they imagined them, and so quickly set off. Soon they reached a little town, most of which seemed to be—was, in fact—an old-fashioned amusement park, replete with all manner of rides, many of which, like the Tunnel of Love and the Ferris Wheel, struck the travelers as quaint, and perhaps pointless. They were, however, pleased, although Louise was embarrassed when a jet of air, suddenly released from a hole in the floor over which she was standing unawares, blew her skirt up around her waist. Her blushes pleased a leering clown who was, apparently, "in charge" of the air jet. The mountains seemed to be just outside the town, although it became apparent that the town was deep within the mountains. "Perhaps *this* is the excursion," Alex said.

Later, after a lunch of hot dogs and cotton candy, they agreed to separate so as to "explore" the amusement park and environs, and to meet later in the day by a ride called the Big Lasso, and Basil, Harry, and Anna left. Alex looked around for Louise but she had gone somewhere without so much as a word. At the hour appointed for their rendezvous, Alex obediently stood before the Big Lasso, but nobody showed up, so he spend much of the afternoon watching ferries sail to and from Platinum Carde Island, out in the middle of a startlingly turquoise-colored artificial lake. He felt abandoned and hurt, especially when, later, they returned and asked him where he'd *been* all day. He turned away, reddening with anger.

Harry told him to "hop" into his convertible, which he called, for some reason, "Jewish blue," and said that he'd always wanted to see the Sixty-ninth Street pier in Brooklyn, from which, he'd read, *real* ferryboats once made regular runs to and from Staten Island, at the time wholly unpopulated save for a few dozen Boy Scouts who had been forbidden to return to the "mainland" because of sexual thoughts that they had been unable to suppress despite prayers and chats with their ministers and coaches: they were no longer "clean" or "reverent," or so *Boys' Life* reported. Harry turned onto Sixty-ninth Street and headed for the pier.

But once outside the car a few steps found them in a field of mud through whose gluey expanse they had to slog before they could reach the pier, which they could see quite clearly ahead of them; it was crowded with people, and drenched with spray from the very rough waters of the Narrows. They scraped the mud off their shoes and walked, finally, onto the pier. Basil, Louise, and Anna were sitting at a table under an umbrella, drinking beer. Basil lifted a glass in exaggerated greeting. "My beer is Rheingold, the dry beer," he said. "Think of Rheingold whenever you buy beer." "You never intended to meet at the Big Lasso," Alex said. "You spent the whole day *here!*" Harry shook his head and told Alex to relax. "We were not here all day at all," he said, "You think everything is an excursion." Anna laughed drunkenly, but then gave Alex a threatening look. "He's *always* thought everything's an excursion. This whole dumb idea is his, isn't it?" Alex realized that he'd lost his shoes. "Look!" he said. "Look! Look! Who's going to buy me some new shoes? These were Flagg Brothers square-toe loafers, dyed cordovan!" He was overwhelmed by a childish rage. "You never *intended* to meet at the Lasso," he said. "What *friends!*" They all looked at him, amused yet slightly annoyed. "Oh well, " Basil said. "What a beautiful day it is anyway, right?"

— XXXV —

He and his wife of a little more than a year decided to give a New Year's Eve party for their closest friends, another recently married couple: it would just be the four of them. They were, then, surprised to find that their friends had brought along a man from the husband's office, Zoltan, whom the husband described as his "partner." He seemed a rather inconsequential figure, pale and faded. He sat on one end of the sofa and began to drink bourbon and water, steadily, and with a kind of sincere devotion to the whiskey. The hostess had what she would have called—had she been asked—a "bad feeling" about him.

It became clear to the host, despite the blurring of his thought by alcohol, that Zoltan had sexual designs on his co-worker's wife, who pretended to be blind to his unconcealed desire. That she permitted her skirt to ride up to her thighs testified to her awareness, even though she worked so as to seem blithely careless. It was, after all, New Year's Eve, she might have said. Zoltan ogled her thighs with an ardor just slightly less pronounced than his love for his whiskey, but this was allowed to pass by all. Who can tell why? Relationships, as they now call them, faint, stumble, and collapse every day because of such social niceties: all Zoltans seem to know this, with the instinct of animals.

Sometime just before midnight, when the little party had become somewhat waywardly morose despite the good-times Ray Charles recording that nobody had the will to dance to, the doorbell rang, and the visiting wife, the guest, assuming the hostess's duties, opened the door to Jake, an old friend of both husbands. He stood there smiling, a quart of Scotch in each hand, his coat flung carelessly over his shoulders. He put the Scotch on the floor and took his friend's wife in his arms, then kissed her, as they say, passionately, his mouth open, as was hers. He had his hands as low on her waist as he, perhaps, dared, but his intentions were very clear. His candor seemed merely his attempt to disguise them with "honesty."

Zoltan got up from the couch, and lurched toward the couple, patting, in some absurd gesture of comfort, his host's shoulder on the way to the door. He pulled Jake away from his "partner's" wife and then pushed his mouth into hers, lewdly, slobbering, grunting, rubbing his hands up and down her thighs. Her husband got up, very calmly, walked to the couple, and kicked his wife in her buttocks before pulling her around to face him; then he slapped her face and slapped her face again. The record had ended, and as if caught in the perfect web of the perfect cliché, the voices of people in the street were suddenly clear in their strained and vaguely hysterical revelry.

The husband yanked and pulled his wife over to the sofa and sat her down, then looked at his old friends, and sneered at them. "Here's your fuckin' *friend!*" He opened the closet door and pulled out his overcoat and Zoltan's, while Jake stood in the open doorway, in something more than shock—did he really *know* these people? The husband gave Zoltan his coat, put his on, and picked up one of the bottles of Scotch Jake had put on the floor what seemed like hours before. "I'm not interested in you people anymore," he said. "I'll call you soon, bitch," he said to his wife. Then he pushed Zoltan out the door and followed him, leaving the door open: they began quarreling as they went down the stairs.

"Jesus," his wife said. "Jesus." She sat sprawled on the sofa, her legs apart; both men stared at her, embarrassed. The hostess gave her a glass of straight bourbon and roughly, angrily yanked her skirt down her thighs. "Keep your skirt down!" she said. "You *child.*"

— XXXVI —

The professor had made a small but firm reputation as a translator of late nineteenth-century French poets, the lesser lights, so to speak, most especially Laforgue and Corbiere, of the great Modernist explosions of the age. His translations were quietly celebrated as definitive "for our time."

It may not be surprising to note that the professor, in his youth, had been an aspiring poet, but his talents were meager and so he moved resolutely, yet with a somewhat bohemian show of the devil-may-care, through his education, earning his PhD at the age of twenty-eight, and starting the nerve-wracking process of "getting settled," i.e., being granted tenure. The professor did not quite think of himself as an academic, but as an artist, and perhaps, in his own vaguely deluded way, he was. He may have silently vowed the physician's vow: first, do no harm.

He ultimately got tenure at a mediocre state university, where his colleagues in the comparative literature program were to grow jealous of his small fame (an article in the *Chronicle of Higher Education* had included his name and a few lines on his translations in an article on "poet professors" it was noted that his work was "dazzlingly eccentric," yet "sound in its meticulous scholarship").

His scholarly career had been "checkered," for from an undergraduate interest in the "silver" or "drab" poets of the early English renaissance, he moved, unexpectedly, into an enthusiastic—or so it appeared—study of Aubrey Beardsley, Oscar Wilde, *The Yellow Book*, etc.; in short, the English Decadence. It was rather stale stuff, but the book he made of it—and which earned his tenure—caused a stir because of his carefully ingenious argument that a pornographic homosexual novel anonymously published, ca. 1895, *Teleny*, was written by Oscar Wilde. His comparison of the style with that of *Dorian Gray* was somewhat strained, but "unusual and "daring," especially in the argument that conflated the protagonists of both novels as the same depraved dandy. But that was that—the English Decadence, the professor learned, led nowhere but to a lifetime in, let's say, northern Iowa. That would never do.

And so he moved, with some flattery, here and there, some to-ing and fro-ing and faculty lunches and dinner parties, into the outer precincts of the romance languages department, and Vallejo became the center of his new book, a neohistorical study of the imagery in *Trilce*, that got him an offer from a very good private university, after which it was adiós to

Vallejo, and the French poets were suddenly hauled from the wings, where they had, perhaps, been sitting for some time with Max Beerbohm and the Earl of Surrey.

In his new post, he modestly requested of the creative writing program if he might teach a course in literary translation, under its auspices of course, and his growing celebrity made this a cinch, especially since he offered to teach it in addition to his regular course load. So there he was, a writer, in effect, at last. He was very much "like" a writer, even, with his beret and faded denim shirts, his bicycle and worn corduroys. Well.

He married a graduate student some two years later, a washed-out young woman of great sensitivity, who made a first-play splash with a little one-acter called *¡Ay Caramba!* "Its intermittent sizzle comes from its winningly disingenuous juxtaposition of Hebrew linguistics, Twelve-Step dogma, the CIA, and the ties between them," asserted the *Village Voice*, with guarded enthusiasm. They are both middle-aged now, and the professor's wife has all but given up writing and has begun showing her photographs at a "discriminating" gallery in town. The professor now teaches but one course a semester, a freshman seminar in the English Decadence, in which he assigns his own book, self-deprecatingly, to be sure. He loves the fact that his bluntly sexual chapter on *Teleny* makes his students look at him with a surprised respect. And, not to forget, he is writing poetry again, and publishing it in the literary magazine of the English department, *Redwood Review.*

— XXXVII —

H e'd finally got a job checking freight for the King
Assembly Agency, working on a North River platform of the Pennsylvania Railroad, with whose
checkers and car loaders the assembly agency
worked in tandem.

The weather had grown increasingly colder as January
progressed, and one morning, as he walked into the violent
wind blowing up Fortieth Street from the river, he knew that
this day, the first truly cold day on his new job, would be
astonishingly cruel. And so it was.

His marriage had been steadily disintegrating, even
though it was barely more than a year old. His wife looked at
him, or so he thought, with a passive, almost friendly, benign
contempt, although he had no idea why: perhaps he was
wrong. He certainly could not have furnished any "proof" or
examples of this contempt, but it was there, he knew. It was
there. He believed that one day soon he'd be given a sign of

some sort to prove, to his satisfaction, that his wife happily despised him, and always had, that their marriage was teetering on the edge of collapse, and that she was ready to take advantage of any catalyst to give it a careless push.

Al, the foreman, took a look at him in his absurdly inadequate clothing, and gave him a woollen watch cap to pull over his ears, his ears and his stupid head, the head of what Al had, on this bitter day, called, dismissively, a "college boy." The cap kept his head from freezing, but did nothing for his body or his feet, numbed into two chunks of icy flesh from the frigid concrete floor of the platform. This was his true initiation into the world of brutally hard work, "honest," as they say, work.

The sign would arrive and he would see it or feel it deeply; there would be no doubt of it. Then, only then, armed with this certainty, he could confront his wife and ask her to tell him the truth. The truth. Perhaps, he occasionally thought, she wasn't aware of how she treated him, how she talked to him with equal measures of impatience and patronization, wasn't aware of how she was to him. His candor would awaken her own, and perhaps *something* would be made clear between them, and "things" might then be brought cleanly to a conclusion, before both of them were drained of their youth and what was left of their honesty. It never occurred to him that if his wife consciously acted toward him in the manner he thought—he knew—she did, that she might like it, that she might like doing this to him, that she had married him so that he would always be near, waiting patiently to be insulted and demeaned.

On the following day he would wear long underwear, put a few sheets of newspaper between two sweaters, and don a scarf, the cap that Al had given him, heavy gloves, and two pairs of socks under his old low quarters. He would be a worker instead of a chump, sad in his chump's ignorance.

On the evening of that first bleak and bitter day, when he took himself home, a core of terrible ice sat solid inside his body; all the way home on the subway, the bus, the three-block walk to the small apartment that he and his wife were slowly fading away in, he shook with the cold. A glass of straight bourbon couldn't get him warm, nor could the spaghetti, of which he had seconds and then thirds. It did nothing. He trembled and shook at the table and while he watched television and, undressing for bed, shook even more fiercely as the cool air of the bedroom touched his bare flesh. And then he realized that *this* was the sign, this frozen center of his body, his pitiful, stupid body was her body, too: they were both dead or dying. His wife asked him, for the first time, what the matter was. She smiled as if vaguely annoyed by the intolerable ague that possessed him. Are you *sick?* she asked. Oh yes, he was indeed.

— XXXVIII —

He was a third-rate painter, who believed, because he had started painting as a ten-year-old in England, that he had been born a kind of prodigy, of the sort that simply could not blossom in the United States. When he came to America at fifteen, with his mother and father, he was enrolled in public high school, where his meager talents impressed his teachers, whose knowledge of painting had been gleaned from worn postcards from the Met and Modern, the Art Institute of Chicago, the Frick, and so on. They knew that their pupil was—what *was* he?—he was far more talented and knowledgeable than anyone else in their classes or in the school, for that matter. All this praise and blather enforced his fantastic conception of himself. So his adolescence and young manhood passed, and at twenty-two or so he was turning out canvases that were banal parodies of de Kooning. In this, it must be said, he was not alone. He was quite insufferable in every way, suffused, as he was, with monstrous illusions of his restless and iconoclastic genius, although one had to know him for a time before these aberrations showed themselves plain.

It so happened that he met a beautiful and funny and intelligent girl at one of the scores of parties that tended to erupt, acne-like, in the downtown "scene" of the mid-fifties, those carnival days. To the astonishment of everyone, he and this girl began an affair, and, six months later, married. It seemed clear that she married him because of what she took to be his genius and because of her devotion to this genius; and he married her because she—only properly—flattered him and, well, she was beautiful. "See?" he seemed to say to his peers, all of them peering out enviously from behind their inert versions of "Bill" and "Franz" and "Jackson." She was, as noted, intelligent and educated, but basically ignorant of art when she married the whiz. But. Ah, but.

But her marriage to him brought her, quite naturally, into contact with many artists on an almost daily basis—dinners, shows, openings, parties, weekends in the Hamptons before the sands had turned to gold dust, raucous and drunken Provincetown softball games, and so on. And these painters, as well as their wives and lovers, said enough, usually obliquely and glancingly, but enough, to let her know that they thought of her man as, well, not much of an artist, and a bit of a bore. Even more damaging to the connubial partnership, she began to: 1) see the work of good, sometimes very good, painters who were her husband's peers; and 2) develop a critical eye, a set of aesthetic measures, a way of thinking about painting that was independent of her husband's essentially envy-tainted remarks. And so she began to see clearly his work, and to battle with herself over what she thought to be her growing, silent betrayal of him. But he was, well, he was, really, not very good. Not very good at all.

Slowly, softly, and as they say, as quietly as the famous little cloud no bigger than a man's hand, she began to think of him differently and then to treat him differently; she moved from a kind of genial tolerance to vague patronizing denigrations to blunt contempt. After two years, she left him. He continued to paint, of course, but his anger and unhappiness did nothing for his work, which, in point of fact, got worse. This was the period in which he did a series of what he called "Suburb" paintings, about which even his friends were uncomfortably silent. Some of these daubs were hung on the walls of new restaurants in the newly named SoHo; later, he moved to England, where his career foundered and collapsed.

— XXXIX —

heldon Dufoy's letter to last week's "Faith Base" section was in very poor taste and lacking of good sense and education in the Christian religion field. The Bible tells all Christians who are true Christians that there is no way of entering Heaven unless you are born again and accepting Jesus Christ in your heart as the only true Lord of the Universe, be it vast or otherwise, it does not matter for the Lord God is all Supreme.

There is no other god or gods, and Mohammed (or Allah), Moses, Talmud, Buddha, Zen, Hindu Deity, and others, for instance, of the Eskimos, Africans, Bushmen, Pygmies, and so on are, are all false gods that lead nowhere but to everlasting torture in the fiery flames of Hell forever in eternity, Mr. Dufoy's secular humanistic beliefs and fashionable liberal ideas are not based on the Holy Bible, which alone, he might not be aware of, is the Word of God.

As for the translation of God's word maybe being not accurate and so, therefore, not the true Word of God, as was spoken by Him or Jesus Christ, his son, Mr. Dufoy should know, to lighten up his ignorance, that the Almighty God or Jesus sometimes was at the side of King James and his helpers as they labored, in spirit and giving them strength in their labors. It is almost amusing to read such displays of ignorance however, but I hope that Mr. Dufoy soon asks God into his heart, for Jesus, is always standing by miraculously every single person at the same time, waiting for such an invitation, even though it may be given by a Jewish person, despite what they have done to Him over the thousands of years ever since Adam and Eve. He forgives even them and their crucifixion of Him, hard though it is for, He is the lord of forgiveness and a great Boss, no matter how small it may seem or unimportant.

This letter was found in the desk drawer of its author some few weeks after a massive stroke led to his death outside the Pinto movie theater, which establishment he had just exited. The film playing at the time was *Hot Bottoms*, starring J'Adore Vegas. The letter was tucked into an addressed, stamped, but not sealed envelope. In another drawer of the same desk there was discovered some 1,500 pages of pornographic writings by the same author, rife with solecisms, tattered grammar, bad spelling, and a syntax seemingly borrowed from a lost language.

Notable in this work of erotica—apparently a series of linked amorous adventures—is the presence of a recurring female character, a "quivering," "shameless," "tremballing," "moaning," "large-breasted," and "full-lipsed" young woman, who, the patient reader is told, over and over again, looks exactly like Julia Roberts, and who often has "depraved" and "perverted" sex with other women, all of whom bear the name of the deceased author's wife, Myrna.

When told of the discovery of this venereal cache, Myrna unhesitatingly averred that Satan was certainly the author of such filthy material, for her husband—and, as his wife, she could, she said, testify to this—knew absolutely nothing about sex. "I could tell you some stories," she remarked, and then fell silent.

Satan's evil literature was burned at a ceremony conducted by the White-Robed Ladies of the choir of the Lamb's Blood Ministries, Inc., Church, in the parking lot, to cries of "Amen!," "Jesus!," and "Yes!," wails of joy, and the loud clashing of tambourines. The purification ceremony was followed by a buffet luncheon in the church's basement, where the pastor, Ellsworth Roy Womp, noticed how her White Robe flattered Myrna's figure.

— XL —

He is driving his father's Fleetwood sedan to the latter's house, which is near a beach that he somewhat imprecisely recalls. He is driving because his father, while he seems to be strong and alert, is an old man who has had some minor road accidents of late, "moving violations," as they are officially called. But when he stops to get gas, his father, without a word, gets behind the wheel and takes over the driving.

After traveling perhaps ten or twelve miles, his father turns the Cadillac off the highway into a sparsely wooded area from which a faint dirt road leads into scrub woods and dry grass. His father, without hesitation, takes this road, and suddenly accelerates, so that they are traveling at high speed. He has the idea, which comes to him calmly, that his father wants to kill both of them and he understands why, but says nothing. His father is smiling, pleased and smug and oddly youthful in manner and appearance.

The car bursts out of the woods and the dirt road suddenly becomes a well-paved one, smooth and straight. It appears to be the main street of a small, falsely picturesque seaside town, quaint shops and art galleries seemingly everywhere. Yet on their right is a carton-like building made of gray concrete slabs, some ten stories tall, and in the final stages of construction. On a sixth-story scaffolding, a construction worker is performing oral sex on what seems to be a businessman, who bites the handle of his briefcase in sexual pleasure. The building, in its fierce ugliness, is wholly out of place in the cutely fake little town. A sign near the outdoor freight elevator reads NEPTUNES BAYE ESTATES. His father ignores the building and remarks that this is a very nice town, clean and quiet and right on the water, even though the people who live here are for the most part disgusting fanatic Christians who believe that God speaks to them. At the end of the street lies a glistening stretch of what looks to be a bay edged by a strip of white sand. "Look how the clear blue water sparkles and glitters!" his father says. "Just the place for the family to kick back and *enjoy!* Work? What's that?" He looks at his father in astonishment.

They reach the end of the street and his father makes a left, to continue driving, now parallel to the dazzling beach, which is comfortably crowded with people taking the sun or moving into the calm waters to wade or swim. "You can keep your fabled New Jersey," his father says, looking at the beach. Among the people at the water's edge are, surprisingly, a number of men who are fishing, casting their lines as fishermen do everywhere. He says to his father that it seems a strange place to fish, since whatever fish may possibly have been in the water hereabouts are most certainly gone, driven away by all the splashing and clamor. His father replies that these fish are used to noise and people and don't mind a bit, they come close in to shore to eat the leftover food that the people invariably cast into the water, "actually, surf," his father says. "Don't be surprised, by the way, to learn that the construction worker back there is really a famous movie star." Just then, one of the fishermen's lines goes taut with an obvious strike, and he finds that he is very pleased.

They get out of the car and sit under some trees at the edge of the beach farthest from the water. He says that he remembers that his father landed the largest blue marlin ever caught off the Florida coast, and his father smiles and nods, delighted that his son has remembered this. He says that he told one of his students about his father's catch and that she was very impressed. His father is looking at him with tender, impossibly tender love, and he feels, at that moment, overwhelming, crushing sadness and loss, deep and irremediable, and he begins to cry and wakes, crying.

— XLI —

l's wife had left him for a casual friend, the owner of a chain of bathroom-furnishings stores in the Midwest—a man whom Al had always casually despised. He was unprepossessing in every way— short, dumpy, with thick-lensed glasses, a high, whining voice, bow legs and acne scars. His sense of humor was so perfectly blunted that it seemed as if he had been born with an "a-comedic" gene. To make his lack of graces and charm even more pronounced—at least to Al—he had, as a Jew, no sense of or interest in his putative religion, yet had become a passionate, even slightly crazed defender of Israel, as if that state's fortunes and security had something important to do with his gray life. To listen to him "on Israel," was, according to Al, to be trapped in a weird Jackie Mason monologue, sans timing or even that performer's weary shtick. Al thought of his rants as "enoughness already."

After Al and Ginny's divorce become final, it became clear to him—or, let us say, he admitted it to himself with qualification, that she had married Norman Shin Bet for his money. That he had earlier refused to consider this seriously, as they say, may reveal the "credit" that he gave his wife's motives; perhaps she really did love the grotesque? But no, it was the money, it had to be the money. Her—Al's and her— two daughters were now attending private schools in Westchester, they took riding lessons and were both on a brilliantly snobbish swim team that practiced in an Olympic-size pool when they weren't sneering at everything and pretending not to be Jewish. As for Ginny, the last time he had seen her, when she'd come to pick up the girls from his rat-trap apartment on Avenue A, she was wearing a tweed coat as beautifully tailored as it was exquisitely soft and elegantly draped, and a pair of knee boots of dark-brown velvety suede. How he loathed her, how he loathed her coat and her boots and her goddamned smug, suddenly different, rich face.

His attitude became darker and more acidic as time passed. He no longer cared that he'd lost his bitch whore of a wife and his two snotty daughters, nor did he care that she'd left him for the Frog King, the fucking Jew bastard, the sweaty kike whose family, Al *knew*, had smelled of stale sweat and fish before the money rolled in. What he cared about was that *she* had got the money and he'd got *nothing!* And yet he'd been ordered to pay child support to her and Norm, miserable Norm! They must have laughed themselves sick whenever his pitiful check arrived in the mail. "The measly check is here!"

he'd no doubt say, the fat little prick! "Ha ha ha! How *will* we ever spend it all? Shrimp lo mein?"

One day, Al bought three gallons of the darkest green paint that he could find in Kamenstein's, Forest Green, although it was truly the color of hell. Over the course of two or three days, he painted his entire apartment, including the ceilings, this sepulchral green, a green so gloomy and bleak that it seemed the representation of utter despair, a suicidal color, if one can call it a color, for it was somehow blacker than black. Those friends he had left—those few who could tolerate his rantings about the goddamn Jews this and the fucking kike bastards that—made no mention of what was this anteroom of insanity. A remark here and there by Al seemed to indicate that he had stepped into that state, although he said that he had "changed" his apartment to assure himself that he was not *yet* mad; for if the rooms filled him with dread, that dread was, so he said, a sign of hope that he would one day come to terms with the hurt that had been done him: if he could stand living here, he could stand anything. He suggested that the vile darkness of his place gave him a frisson of—what?—life, perhaps. Nothing could be worse than the wretchedness that he had constructed to enclose him. He was not yet dead if he could survive this tomb.

— XLII —

Here is a man, placed, when he was but eight years old, into an orphanage by his father, a man overwhelmed by the necessity of raising, alone, three children, while denying, for a year and a half, the fact that his wife had gone totally insane. The boy was selected, so to say, by his father, on what can only be called a whim. And so off he went to the orphanage, while his siblings lived on with their father in the small frame house in Troy. He was more or less ignored by his family, and after a few years, forgotten.

In 1942, he was permitted to leave the orphanage, a year earlier than decreed by law, so that he could join the army, which he discovered to be very much like the orphanage. He fought through Europe with the Second Armored Division of Patton's Third Army, was wounded three times, and was discharged early in 1945, on points. After holding a job as an assistant manager in a relative's floor-covering business, he enrolled, for some wholly obscure reason, in a Baltimore art school, and the moment he put a brush to canvas, knew what he was meant to do with his life, his time, with everything. The paint would occult, with color and texture, his family, silently; perhaps even kill them. And so he became a painter.

His relationships with women were ephemeral and unsatisfactory. He wanted to be humiliated, embarrassed, shamed—he wanted to be dominated, but his desires were far removed from the carnal. He wished to be erased. It was, or so he must have thought, all he was good for, as hopeless as he was, as unhappy as he was, as useless as he was. In the orphanage, ignored by his father and his hateful siblings, and unremembered by his crazy mother, he had seen the routine sadisms of the institution as small deliverances. But in the army, through the years of blood and agony and horror, the severed limbs and shit and pus of ceaseless death, he had not even been *present* enough to be killed, to become another cipher. That he became a good painter, a very good painter, meant, of course, nothing, insofar as his happiness was concerned. He was a very good artist choked with misery.

He could not ask the women who passed through his life to shame and debase him, he had no words to ask these things, and, perhaps, he had no true sense of *what* he wanted. He did not avail himself of professional women who could have relieved him, for that would have been different, grossly erotic; he needed someone who cared for him, however fragile that caring might have been, to insult and demean him. He wished to be humiliated by a friend; a gentle friend.

Perhaps with the knowledge that he was sublimating his deepest desires, addressing and satisfying them in some vague and peripheral way, or perhaps not, he chose—this was long before he had a regular dealer or gallery—he chose to make a living by working as a waiter. He complained to everyone he knew about how terrible a job it was, how he loathed it, how he would get back to his studio too exhausted to paint (this was not true), how he'd rather do anything else, and so on. But he loved the work, loved being shouted at by the chefs, the head waiters, the bartenders; he loved being treated contemptuously by so many of the diners, whom he thought of as foul, slobbering pigs, their money earning them a place at the expensive trough and the absolute right to insult and harry this cheap-tuxedo-wearing slave, this lackey, this zero. When he watched them eat, his stomach would turn over with nausea, and he would be obscurely delighted that these swine had power over him.

He loved it, he wanted it. He needed it. It was precisely what he was worth, it was all he was worth. It was a wife and a mistress, troops of luscious whores, all of them waiting to carry out his depraved, self-abasing orders. To be humiliated. To be embarrassed. To be shamed and shamed again to the core of his being. To be salvaged at last and forever.

— XLIII —

Deny it to himself as he would, his work had begun to bore him. Well, he had been at it for fifty years, a little more, really, than fifty years, if he counted apprentice work; he had a shelf of books to attest to those wearying yet absorbing labors, to those thousands of hours, millions of words, and, he was chagrined to recognize, the slow but absolute fading away of what had at one time been a small but definite critical attention to his books. Fifty years. It was indeed wondrous, so he often thought, that he had managed to live at all, to walk and talk and eat and laugh, to love women, to father children—how had that happened?

Perhaps most unsettling—beyond the nagging sense that he had lived but in his spare time—his books, whenever he took one down at random, out of curiosity or to refresh his memory as to how he had managed a specific formal problem, invariably shocked him in that nothing in any of them seemed in the least familiar, but looked as if—read as if—written by a stranger who had secretly invaded his mind and absorbed large quantities of his memories. Worse still, every book—and there they were, with their familiar titles, with his name on jacket and case—every book seemed too good for his talents, such as they were, such as he considered them to be. Who had written this paragraph? these pages? these chapters?—some of which struck him as so artistically authoritative, so perfect, so sublime, that he felt as if he had plagiarized, word for word, the work of another, much better writer.

And so his current work, beyond its somewhat mischievous, even malign capacity to fill him with an ennui so profound as to exhaust him, appeared to him to cast a shadow on his earlier work, to demean it, sully it, in a sense to sabotage it. With every sentence he wrote, it seemed, an earlier sentence, a glittering and suave sentence, decayed a little. But this was all he knew how to do. He wasn't much good for anything else, and what he did know how to do—even when, he smiled ruefully—even when he knew how to do it, proved nothing, changed nothing, and spoke to about as many people as one could fit into a small movie theater.

And so he continued to do it, correcting and revising each newly made page with a feeling of weird neutrality, with a feeling that he was simply passing the time: this or solitaire— all right, this. Surely, the other old writers he still knew felt precisely this way. Did they? He surely wouldn't ask such an impertinent question.

He had recently received a letter from a dear friend, who, it so turned out, died soon after. He took the letter from his files one morning, before he started what he now thought of as "work," scare quotes flaring, and found in it what he was sure he had read. The friend had confessed to him that his last book was, indeed, his *last* book, that he had given up or lost— it made little difference—the ability and the desire to write another word. His friend lamented the fix that he was in, but his frustration seemed forced, it seemed a position taken because of proprieties, the old truisms about art: *a writer who cannot write, how sad, how tragic.* It was a role his friend was playing. So it seemed, so it was.

He sat as his desk, and read the letter again. He wished, oh how he wished it wasn't so, but he was choked with envy of his friend's sterility: not to be able to write, not to want to write, to be, as they say, "written out," or, more wonderfully, "burnt out"—lovely phrase! But it was a gift that had not been given him, and, he knew, despairing, that it would never be given him. He was doomed to blunder through the shadows of this pervasive twilight, until finally, perhaps, he would get said what could never be said.

He'd stopped abusing alcohol years ago, although he disliked the word "abusing," and used it only with people he didn't know or didn't care to know. He thought it a spurious word, a kind of self-help, onward-and-upward, simperingly Christian word that conjured up an image of a frenzied drunk assaulting a bottle of whiskey in a perverse madness. He hadn't "abused" alcohol, but had spent almost four years sitting in a chair drinking jug wine around the clock and looking, variously, at the wall, the window blind, and the TV screen. Now he was sober and had been for more than five years. What he discovered was that being sober meant no more than *being sober:* he certainly was no more content, no more serene, nor had he found anything *wonderful* to fill his "leisure" hours, no God, in whatever costume. He went to work, came home, ate his frozen dinners, drank tomato juice with a lot of tabasco in it, and watched television. He smoked less, but that was because his salary was pitifully low at the prussianly anti-union retail outlet he worked at.

He lived alone, as might be surmised, his three failed marriages having taught him nothing about women or sex or give and take or, for that matter, anything at all. He had no children, thank God, and now, at sixty-eight, fantasies of erotic adventures in which the ex-wives lasciviously collaborated, or substituted for each other, or were blurred together with other insatiable women, real or invented, were his entertainment. Who performed what perversion and when, and how did she do it and where were they all when it happened? It was pitiable entertainment, of course, but he didn't care one way or another; he was concentrated, obsessively, on his self, his actual body and flesh, and he accepted the knowledge that he was sick, not of any disease, but sick of himself, of his self. It surely must be a common ailment, so he thought. How to reach one's late-sixties and not be self-loathing?

He had considered the possibility that he might actually be ill with some spectacular, malignant, fatal disease, lymphoma perhaps, or something even more devastating. Yet the thought of going to "see" his doctor filled him with a boredom and unease strong enough to bring on nausea. For a few years, soon after his last marriage had imploded in slow-motion misery, he'd gone regularly to his doctor, and to other doctors referred to, had tests and more tests, blood panels and urinalysis, examinations and biopsies, for a pain here, a twinge there, irregular bowel movements, fluttery heartbeats, shortness of breath, difficulty sleeping, weak urine flow, and on and on: he had become, that is, an official *patient*, whose responsible job it was to worry about his health and juggle doctors' appointments and ask questions about his medications and their possible side effects (there was one drug that could, it was thrillingly advised, cause a fatal reaction after just one dose!). It was a job much more fulfilling than the one he made $12.43 an hour at, where nobody would look seriously into his face and suggest that he might have chronic prostatitis—or worse.

But one day he realized that no matter how militantly—or weirdly—obsessive he was or would be about his health, he was, at sixty-eight, good for (a nice phrase) maybe ten more years, if that, and then oblivion. It was the neurotic and worried people between thirty-five and forty-five who thought that diet and exercise and meditation and the avoidance of cigarette smoke and excessive alcohol use (alcohol *abuse!*) would keep them from death; and that industrious and puritanical attention to their aging bodies would take them into their happy nineties, their euphoric hundreds, into a deathlessness as groggily sweet as a California chardonnay. Their bodies would *repay* them for their scrupulous care.

He knew better than this, although he considered that he might well be wrong, but, sick of himself, bored with himself, there was no regimen of health to which he could subscribe without embarrassing himself deep within his psyche, or what was left of it. He of course, like any reasonable human being, considered suicide, for who would miss him? But he refused the idea when he thought that perhaps one day an actual terrible, serious, rampaging disease would enter him or awaken within his body where it had been dozing all these years, a disease that he and his doctors could "battle," or, better, "bravely battle," but to which he would at last grudgingly succumb. In the meantime, he decided to start drinking again, to *abuse* alcohol, and with abandon. Christ knows that he'd wanted a drink every hour of every day for years. If he was sick of himself and waiting for the possible declaration within his body of the presence of some malignant destroyer, why not wait drunk?

— XLV —

There once was a man who coveted his friend's wife, and even though he was an Evangelical Christian, complete with closed eyes, raised arms, enraptured visage, and a well-burnished hatred of Satan, and in despite of the ninth commandment, his lust grew and flourished. So much so that he set about, with much sweaty praying in the night for his pal, God's, personal assistance in his travails, seducing the woman. This was not as hard as he thought it might be, for she had a touch of the whore about her. And so he violated the sixth commandment: in for a nickel, in for a buck. After a time, the man had become thoroughly obsessed with the woman, mad for her, as they say, and wished no more than to be inside of her day and night. The woman's husband was oblivious to this sexual carnival. He was the perfect cuckold; he no longer desired his wife, so believed her undesirable to others.

One day, the lovers "ran off" to live together, love together, hump each other crazy, and do this forever and ever, et cetera.

For some reason, they headed in the man's somewhat exhausted car, a nauseatingly green Ford Granada, to his home town, Lawton, Oklahoma. He had been born and raised in this burg, in which his parents and sister, washed in the blood of the lamb, still lived in a clapboard house, "the old homestead," as the whole family liked to call it, smilingly: they might well have been the salt of the earth, or a pinch of it, anyway. The couple fucked their way, delirious and exhausted, through many motels, and on many occasions, pulled off the road to satisfy their enduring itch. They were, it goes without saying, seized by Paphian mania. The birds sang for them, and the sunshine glowed upon their stunned and unsated faces. There had never been a love like this in the history of the world, never.

When they reached Lawton, and the woman had been introduced to Dad, who did and liked as hobbies, and Mom, deeply involved in, and Sis, a member of the Something and the Whatever; and after the shock of this surprise visit to the old homestead, it became almost immediately clear to the folks at home that this somewhat desperate-looking woman of forty or so, in a too-tight sweater and dirty jeans, was not, she was most assuredly not the prodigal's wife; and, soon after, they realized that, even more damning, she was someone *else's* wife. These sinful revelations were squeezed out of the couple over two or three days, the family working as an inquisitorial team, their Christian smiles of love and understanding slowly fading, fading, fading into masks of righteous and gray anger: *sic transit gloria caritatis.* On the third day, the woman got up and sat on the back porch, smoking and looking out over the grim landscape, seemingly good for growing nothing but spite and hatred. She knew that she had already surrendered.

It will probably come as no surprise that the man, the seducer, the lover, he who would sacrifice all or at least some for his Helen, obeyed his family's injunctions, their orders—given him with many tears and prayers by the bushel—to, well, ditch the whore tramp and beg Jesus to forgive him. The next afternoon, while his lover, who had slept on a mattress on the floor of a closet during their stay, was watching an old movie on TV, he came to her, falling to his knees in front of her, weeping and praying, and begged Jesus to forgive them both, and to wash them clean in his Sacred Blood that would always and as well as for all Eternity! She went upstairs, packed her nylon overnight bag, put her dirty clothes in a paper shopping bag, and sat on the floor: she was thirty-nine years old and had been—was it possible?—bewitched.

That night they left for New York, and although they stayed at many of the same motels while en route to Lawton, the chastised sinner slept in bathtubs or in the car, with a pillow, of course, under his noble head, lest Satan steal upon him in the reaches of the night with soft music, delicate perfumes, and filthy images of the recent past. He and the woman spoke to each other, but as if he were a chauffeur to a slightly demented and dying patient. She directed him to an apartment house in Kew Gardens, and he left her standing in front of it, not before hoping that Jesus might enter her heart with his and, and soon. Then he was off, and she looked after the car, hoping that God, any God at all, would see to it that he died in a crash on the way back home. She entered the lobby, and rang the bell of an old friend, long divorced, hoping that she was home and hospitable. Then she'd see about calling her husband to explain—explain? If he even knew she'd left.

— XLVI —

One morning, working fitfully on a story that he knew was not going to be any good, and that each gluey additional phrase made more awkward and unwieldy, and, worse, egregiously literary and *important*, the old writer put his pen down and lit a cigarette, although he had just about completely given up smoking; he had no idea why—oh, to live longer and with zest and verve, and to make happy the health corps.

He was tired, very tired, and too old and immovably marginalized for the story to make any difference to his life: what he had come to, in his mid-seventies, he had come to. He was respected, yes, he had known and been friends with many famous writers and artists, right, he had won a prize here, an award there, sure, odds and ends of distracted attention on the part of the fame machine. His current publisher, a kind of career "literary person," had started his self-important little house with a young woman of very substantial means and a deep love of literature, of course. Their office "suite" was in Yonkers, magically transmuted to Bronxville on their letterhead. Yonkers/Bronxville was less than an hour from the city, so they could keep up (as they said) with things, yet it was quiet and relaxed, removed from the publishing frenzy (as they said) of New York. So they said and said again while they published salutary but soporific books of what one and all agreed was true literary merit. The publisher had spent his life so far working as an editor at two or three of the big mills, and had been responsible for many books of literary merit by many a spear carrier, some of whom had made back their wishful-thinking advances. But now he was an *independent* publisher, backed by his partner's and, it should be known, lover's money. He had left his unhappy wife and spoiled, unhappy children, who were, of course, really bright, for her. She understood him and his needs and hopes. The song goes on.

The new house, eponymously Solomon & Sorel, published, it so turned out, the same sorts of books for which he had been responsible in the frenzied world of Publishing, Inc. They were respectable, they did no harm, they exhibited to a degree the shopworn tropes and humanistic razzmatazz beloved of reviewers ("as if we have lived with these confused characters through their so-human travails," etc.), and they were much like the bunk published by the latest thirty-year-old genius with the fresh eye and astonishing grasp, the one who makes us look anew at literature, but they were, to the chagrin of S&S, destined for the great void. Perhaps soon they'd luck out, although this phrase in its vulgar candor, was not used.

The house—Solomon was the publisher, Sorel the wealthy lover named, in exchange for the rent, "editor-in-chief"— picked up on the old writer, who is as we know currently smoking; they told him that if he didn't have a current publisher—this was but a courtesy comment—S&S would be honored to be his outlet; he was marvelously this and courageous that and unfairly the other thing and tra la la la la. S&S (known already, cruelly, as So-So House) offered him an advance that would, he calculated cynically, cover his rent for not quite two months, an amount so modest, as they had no shame in saying, that it seemed to be a kind of honorarium presented him for being alive.

So they would publish the novel that had been rejected thirty-seven times, and after the novel, a collection of his short stories: with four or five new ones added to the twenty or so he'd published in his lifetime, they'd have a very attractive book, their phrase. The writer agreed, although he knew that he had very little creative juice left. His good early work was all o.p., and when he looked at it, he couldn't recognize any of it as his. His energy had been left in bars and beds, in quarrels and envies, in bitter disappointments. He was written out, and knew it.

Solomon, and Sorel, too, for that matter, presented, over lunch with him, their notions of the possibilities that these two new books would open—he might well, finally, be recognized for the *master* that he was. The old writer listened and smiled, the hot air blowing about him at the table. He knew that his novel would silently appear and slowly disappear; his stories would barely appear and quickly disappear, and Solomon and Sorel would soon discover that he was not quite pleasant enough, not nearly as enthusiastic as he, well, should have been, and then decide that their relationship with him was not all that it should be. So that would be that; the old writer could see all this with ferocious clarity.

But he wrote on, and would write on, bored with his work, bored with himself, bored with pure Solomon and breathless Sorel, bored with the very idea that any of this meant anything at all to anyone at all. Solomon had said that he was hopeful that his "Village novel," as he called *Jaunty Jolly*, might be nominated for one of the more prestigious prizes, the PEN/Faulkner, perhaps? It was about time. Perhaps the NBA? Why not?

The old writer put the yellow legal pad he'd been writing on into a fresh file folder, on which he wrote *Stories*. He'd look at the story tomorrow, although he didn't want to look at words any more, especially his own. But he would, he would. He should have stopped this foolishness years ago, but he didn't know what else to do and he was not quite ready to disappear into dead silence. Not with the PEN/Faulkner waiting! He was almost amused.

— XLVII —

THE PARK

Donnie had gone in to San Antonio with two other soldiers from his advanced training company in Fort Sam Houston's Medical Field Service School. After hours of drinking in one dump after another, and the boisterous, aimless wandering in search of shabby adventure that is the soldier's substitute for leisure, he somehow lost his companions, or they him. He wandered around in the vicinity of the Alamo, and then "found himself," almost literally, on a bench in the middle of a little park, broke and stupid drunk. He hoped that an M.P. or A.P. patrol wouldn't find him, for he was their perfect catch; and he knew, too, that a city cop would be all too happy to arrest him, one of the flood of vermin that daily spoiled the city. His "civilian" clothes of khakis, low-quarters, and a hideously figured shirt—an AWOL shirt, as it was known—would fool nobody: he was most clearly a soldier and a drunken bum. So he sat, breathing deeply, and looking around nervously and fatalistically: he was drunk and broke in the middle of the San Antonio night; what else was there to say? He thought, absurdly, that if he could manage to walk without staggering, he might be able to get to the bus depot, which was, he was certain, not too far; there, he could look like any other dumb soldier waiting to get back to Fort Sam. He had no money, but the main thing now was for him to get off the street.

A man, perhaps five years older than he, was quite suddenly standing in front of him, and he waited to hear the cold command, "Stand up, soldier," but instead heard the man saying that the M.P.'s were due on their rounds through the park any minute and he'd be pinched for sure. Did he have any place to go for the night? He had no place to go, no; no place to go.

THE HOTEL

The man lived or was staying in a room at the Cactus Hotel, an old frame building of three floors on the edge of the West Side, the Mexican district. The place was bleak but clean, as was the room that they entered on the top floor. The mended sheets looked as if they'd been changed recently, and two paper-thin towels on door hooks were not noticeably soiled. There was a bathroom in the hall that served the three or four guests, so to speak, who lived on the floor. He stripped to his briefs and T-shirt in the bathroom, washed with a cake of Lifebuoy that the man had given him, and dried himself with one of the towels, which had a faint aroma of Aqua Velva.

When he got back to the room, the man was in bed and apparently asleep. Sitting at the side of the bed was a small fat man with thick-lensed glasses, wearing a dirty, wrinkled suit and a gray fedora with a ridiculously wide brim. He was talking, rather urgently, to the man in the bed about a movie that, he remembered, had to do with a gangster who had a recurring nightmare about being lost in a rainstorm, a *white* rainstorm, yeah, he was crazy. The man in the bed made no reply. "Do you remember Kay Francis?" he said to Donnie. "She had a little lisp. *There's* a woman whose ass I'd like to fuck." Donnie smiled faintly and got into bed and the fat man asked to look at his feet, and Donnie, although he had no idea why, stuck his legs out. The man examined each toe, then carefully and lovingly licked his soles. Donnie lay there, oddly pleased, amused even, and then the fat man got up and as he turned to leave, said "Kay Francis," and stroked his crotch. The whole scene seemed absolutely natural and even banal. This was the sort of thing that *happened* at the Cactus Hotel, certainly. Donnie got under the sheet and turned out the shadeless lamp at the side of the bed, then lay, staring awake, after a time realizing, although he didn't want to realize it, that he was sexually aroused, that he wanted the man next to him to turn and reach over and touch him, kiss him, do whatever he wanted. What was the matter with him? Two weeks earlier he had fucked three whores in Nuevo Laredo, he certainly wasn't a fag! But he wanted the man to reach over and touch him, *touch* him, and ask him to do things with him. He turned on his side, his face burning with shame and lust. He knew the man was awake and aware of his desires, and knew, too, that all he had to do was make the first move. He lay rigid, astonished and revolted by his erection.

THE MORNING

The man bought them both chili with beans, flour tortillas, and a couple of cold Carta Blancas the next morning in a little Mexican hole in the wall, said he had to get to work, and they shook hands. Donnie felt ill at ease, in the knowledge that the man had surely known of his aberrant desire of the night before, but nothing, of course, was said by either of them, and the little fat man's visit or appearance was as if it had never occurred; it existed as a vague invention.

Donnie walked, losing his way three or four times, to the bus depot and as he got to the entrance a Sergeant First Class with an I Corps patch came out and Donnie asked him if maybe he could spare a buck toward a ticket back to Fort Sam. The sergeant laughed at him: "Walk, you sorry fuck," he said.

Donnie spent the next six hours panhandling while avoiding M.P.'s until he finally had enough money to buy a ticket back to the fort. He got to his barracks about 4:00 p.m.; a couple of semi-drunks were playing rummy on top of a foot locker, drinking Lone Star and eating hot cherry peppers; otherwise the almost silent barracks had that sad, chaotic Sunday look. One of them looked up, and smiled. "Hey, daddy cool—you get you some hot Meskin ass?" Donnie smirked and pumped his fist. "Fuckin' A."

— XLVIII —

Five years before the crash of October 1929, Guy Bonney—the name an Americanization of Gaetano Bonifacio—married Charlotte Briczewicz, a girl of Polish extraction. He'd met her at a "good clean dance" in Saint Rocco's basement, and they began keeping company, as they used to say, soon after. Her family was bitterly unhappy, fearing, perhaps, that the pure Polish blood of their ancient Tarnowski line would be forever tainted. Guy was a Catholic, but . . . On the other hand, Guy's family was accepting of Charlotte, the marriage, and even what they considered to be her strange moralistic family—it's fine to be Catholic, but the Briczewiczes seemed, well, a little crazy? As Mr. Bonifacio said after a visit "All the saintsa pitcha all over the house-a! Madonn'!" They were aware, too, of the slightly disguised bigotry of Charlotte's family toward "Eyetalians," but, perhaps because of their roiled Mediterranean ancestry, figured that since we are all mongrels that it doesn't much matter who marries anybody.

Guy began to do well in the small home-contracting and remodeling business he'd begun with an older brother, Angelo, and soon a son was born to the couple, who were living in a small frame house in Gerritsen Beach. They were happy, more or less, but Charlotte, swayed by her parents and their unrelenting campaign, had begun to feel superior to Guy, and to find many occasions on which to suggest to him that he was, ah, lacking in some of those things that made America a great country for *real Americans*. His father, my God, she often noted as if in passing, could hardly speak English, and even Guy, even Guy had a *faint* accent, not much, but a little. It was sometimes a little embarrassing when they stepped out for the evening with another "nice" couple ("nice" may be read as "refined" Americans). Guy wondered why his supposed accent had never been mentioned before they were married. Well, she was a pretty good wife, despite her growing oddities.

Guy's business had, of course, suffered because of the deepening Depression, but with ingenuity, a little luck, and some contacts he'd made, he got a city contract here, some NRA work there, and so on, and they seemed to be doing just fine. This, it may come as no surprise, annoyed the Briczewicz family, and, for that matter, Charlotte herself, even though she had a new bedroom suite, an electric refrigerator—a Frigidaire!—and a gray Persian lamb coat. The story, which emerged, sluglike, from the muck of her family's gossip, was that Guy—Guytanno!—was some kind of a gangster or something, or that he was mixed up with gangsters; *something* was going on. Wasn't his office on Wolcott Street in Red Hook, where all the Black Hand guineas lived and figured out ways to steal from decent Americans? Them and the kikes? The atmosphere between Guy and his in-laws was not exactly poisonous, but he was made to understand that he'd better "be good" to Charlotte and her little Stanley, even though the poor baby, so they thought, was sadly corrupted; thank God that he was at least blond. It was the Novena that Mrs. Briczewicz had made to the Infant Jesus of Prague that gave them *that* small gift. Well, God had his reasons, but they could be hard to understand.

Guy tried to pay as little heed to this blanket malice as possible, and, in what was a misplaced attempt to persuade his in-laws to warm to him, to convince them that he was a good solid American husband and father, he regularly invited them to dinner with him and Charlotte and the baby. They dined, always, in a restaurant on Forty-forth Street just west of Eighth Avenue, the Milano, to which, it should be said, he drove them in a new Packard that his excellent credit had made it possible for him to buy: they looked wisely at each other as they settled into its rear seat. His "mom" and "dad" always accepted these invitations, for Charlotte had made it clear to them that they needn't worry that the Eyetalian family would accompany them: *she* had to suffer their loud hospitality once a month at their house in Bath Beach, and she'd let Guy know, *indeed*, that that was enough! His in-laws despised the fact of the Milano almost as much as they despised the fact of the Packard, but most of all, they were angry that Guy had the money to pay for these dinners! Where did he *get* this money? Nonetheless, they packed the food in, from the antipasto through the cannoli and espresso with anisette, complaining that this "spicy Eyctalian food" would, as always, give them terrible heartburn. "It's just like all Eyetalian food," Mrs. Briczewicz said, with wondrous regularity. "You'd think that after being in this country all these years they'd learn how to cook the right way." She would shake her head at such barbarian intransigence.

Charlotte's family—and Charlotte as well—refused to pronounce the name of the restaurant correctly, even though they had heard Guy, as well as various waiters and the owner, say the word many times. They called it the MY-LANNO, seeming to savor the disappointed look on Guy's face. He'd corrected them the first few weeks, and then realized what was being done: this was a subversive marginalization of him. MY-LANNO was an *American* word, or should be. Period. And so Guy, without calling attention to it, began to say "MY-LANNO" as well, and was aware of the smug contempt of Charlotte and her parents in their easy victory.

Now he had lost, one might say, virtually everything but his business, and had become just another dim, wayward American—or so he perhaps regretfully thought. But Charlotte was still his, still blond and blue-eyed, still nice to look at. It wasn't really important to be what he had once been. Was it? "Are you and Sophie free for dinner Sunday at the MY-LANNO?" he'd ask his father-in-law. Who would pause to think about his answer, oh yes, pause to think about it.

illy and his wife, Audrey, were vegetarians, and, like many people who embrace what they consider to be salutary and superior modes of behavior, they, in their perfection, slowly yet relentlessly marginalized all those friends who were not of their dietary persuasion. In this, they were, perhaps, much like cultists, whose happily demented myths make them smugly exclusionary. As the years passed, and up to their elbows in brown rice and tofu, they made many new friends of their ilk, of course.

When one first met Billy, who was a routing clerk for UPS, it seemed, for some reason, that he "did" something interesting: something artistic, perhaps; or excitingly political—shadowy, vague, radical. He wore a long, well-trimmed beard, round wire-rim glasses, and smoked a lot of marijuana, which he was candid but not too candid about—as if it wasn't really worth hiding, yet just lawless enough to keep from the unanointed, the squares. To be enlightened as to his smoking habits was to feel—or at least, many people felt themselves to be—intimate adepts. After knowing Billy a little while, however, it became clear that what he "did" was work as a routing clerk for UPS and stay half-stoned at all times. Still, his rickety "mystique" (such were the times) somehow prevailed, amid the smoke and the perfected ravings of the Stones, the Dead, the Airplane, and other assorted multimillionaire rebels. He was a UPS routing clerk, yes, and nothing else, but he was so perfectly hip that it still *seemed* as if there was something secret and darkly interesting about his life, though it was, metaphorically speaking, a life that possessed the quality of a paper bag.

Audrey was a large, hefty, yet rawboned woman of a startling homeliness: she wasn't ugly or deformed; her features were regular, as they say, but there was a blank neutrality to her face, a kind of dumb look, and her body, oddly enough, seemed to be dumb as well, if that makes any sense. Those who know Audrey will understand this. She deferred to Billy in all things, and was given to small, consciously half-suppressed smiles when some fringe idea—political, artistic, sexual—was mentioned over the broccoli-rutabaga casserole, as if the mysterious Billy knew all about such things, was involved in such things, had, perhaps, thought up such things. She contributed to Billy's phantom panache by herself pretending that he "did" something. For all I know, she may well have thought that Billy *had* a secret, romantic life that he kept from her so as to protect her and their snug domesticity. Where he got the time to lead this life, she would not explore, for when he was not at the UPS job, he was usually at home, cannabis-paralyzed, his ears wide open to the music on their stereo. Rock on, man!

Audrey began attending a macramé class at a nearby community college (Macramé: Fun and Function), and began a small friendship with a woman, some fifteen years her junior, who expressed fascination and delight at the fact that Audrey was a vegetarian, and mentioned, more than once, that she had long considered abandoning meat. Things went along, and Audrey invited her to dinner a few weeks later, at which she and Billy seemed to get along very well. She *loved* the dinner—eggplant, tomatoes, fresh corn, and yellow squash made into a kind of pedestrian ratatouille, salad, carrot cake—one of Audrey's specialties—and herb tea. Billy suggested that he "did"—oh, it's not, he hinted, important—this and that, and Akina, the new friend, was deeply impressed by the reticence of the really interesting Billy. Audrey, of course, helped the scene along, as always: smiles, silences, the works.

They began seeing a lot of Akina, a small, dark woman who wore, more often than not, a strained, worried expression, as if she were about to be interrogated, and whose light-coffee complexion appeared to be—how to put this?—manufactured. Perhaps it was. It was summer now, and when the three went to the beach, Akina, who couldn't swim, seemed either unaware or uncaring that a profusion of her black pubic hair flourished wildly at either side of her bathing suit's crotch. This sight may have maddened Billy, for soon he and Akina were committing adultery with, as they say, abandon, and soon Billy moved out, leaving Audrey hurt and bewildered.

Billy left his job at UPS, at Akina's urging, so that he could "do" all the things that he was capable of; she had realized, of course, that Billy could do nothing at all, but she thought that with his—with his what?—he would make a really great life for them both. Billy had some money, slyly saved in a bank account unknown to Audrey, and they lived off that and the few dollars Akina made working in a boutique on St. Mark's Place, just then beginning its ascent into the diligently fake disreputability it would soon attain. He ignored Audrey's pleas for financial help, smoked more "dynamite weed" than ever, and, with Akina's urging, began to eat meat again: vegetarianism was for dumb fucks—like Audrey! They did a lot of laughing over their lamb chops.

Audrey knew that Billy would tire of Akina, re-embrace his lost, mysteriously vacant life, and return home to her. She suggested that this sort of thing had happened before and that she was, always, to blame for Billy's sexual escapades, and that they had been mutually planned. She smiled Billy's secret smile, his I-can't-talk-about-it smile, and lighted a cigarette made of some sort of rank legume. "Billy," she said, "well . . . Billy." Then she changed the subject; she, and it, obscured in a cloud of smoke that smelled very like a burning barn.

— L —

He didn't understand Los Angeles. It seemed to him a demented collection of buildings scattered haphazardly over a vast area. This lack of understanding was profoundly intensified by the fact that he not only was unable to drive, he had no sense of direction. The old friends from New York with whom he and his restive and discontented wife were staying, took them here and there during their two-week visit, but his pale role as complaisant passenger made the city even more lavishly and bewilderingly strange, for he was never able to locate or isolate or even remember anything that might have served as a landmark, and only knew where he was moments before his host turned into the street where his little cottage stood behind a scrubby lawn that ran directly to the curb with no sidewalk intervening, a commonplace, as he discovered, in California: a place with no sidewalks: pedestrians knew just where they stood.

Perhaps this sense of disconnection, this topographical anomie, contributed to his emotional desuetude, his stunned vacancy, when his wife abruptly left him one sunny, blue Los Angeles day, with a man she had met at a party they'd attended, a man whose name he didn't know nor face remember: a nonentity, if it came to that. The note she left for him was cheerful, even breezy, as if he had been in on the whole affair and had helped plan it. But he soon realized that he, too, had become a nonentity, now that his wife had left him, that he had "lived," so to speak, only in relation to her and her curiously blithe selfishness. His host and hostess were enormously kind to him, and took great care not to seem pitying, although this care was in itself a form of pity, as he and they knew. He was, perhaps, made more contemptible to himself as he thought, as he knew, that the man who had stolen—as he had come to think of it—stolen his wife, did not know *his* name or face either; he could clearly hear his wife's voice: "Oh, what do *you* care what his name is? Take me away!" His face burned with the cuckold's shame.

He spent two week's after his wife's departure drinking steadily, one might say stupidly; he drank until he passed out, began drinking again when his brain flickered awake, then drank until he passed out—this went on and on, and half-permitted him to think that he didn't know what had happened to him: well, he *didn't*. After he sobered up, he left Los Angeles, defeated and dulled, to return to New York on a Trailways bus so as to grind himself into his misery a little more, a little deeper; a man of perhaps fifty in the seat next to him performed fellatio on him in the dark early morning somewhere near Joliet, and he absurdly thought that he was getting even with his wife, the bitch. *Someone* liked him, even if it was this sad old cocksucker.

But New York was of no help, it didn't feel at all like home to him, it existed in a kind of aquatic grayness of sleet and dark clouds and sympathetic friends, all of whom performed their parts as carefully as possible, rarely bringing up his wife save once in a while, to call her a bitch, a whore, even, transgressively, a cunt. He stayed with two of these friends, a man and wife, and in the comically sad way in which life crawls and stumbles its way through time, this couple had always been thought of by their passive guest with a kind of jolly but mocking contempt: now he slept on their pull-out Carlyle couch, ate their food, and drank their liquor.

He began to talk to them about his wife, to confide in them, to think of them as the intimate friends that they assuredly were not. In his neurotic and uxorious gloom, he said, in many different ways, the same thing over and over to them: *Where is my wife? I want my wife!* He would take her back no matter what, ask her nothing, forgive her everything, she could walk on him, kick him, she could spit on him! if only she would come back to him, come back and make him the complete slave and idiot of abasement that he so longed to be. His was a continuing performance that went beyond humiliation, a groveling masochism of which he embarrassingly seemed fully aware. They watched him in silence as he blubbered and wailed; it was horrifying. But not to him.

A week or two into the crazed life that he was sedulously creating for himself, he found out, somehow, that his wife and her kidnapper, her rapist, her Svengali and sinister sexual magician, her depraved wizard, her slavering satyr with his enormous phallus eternally ready for her, only her . . . he found out that they were living in St. Louis. He had no address for them, and no way of thinking them—of thinking her—into the landscape: what did St. Louis look like? But he unexpectedly got the address from his host, who had a friend in St. Louis, an assistant professor at Washington University. He had no idea how any of this had come about.

He wanted to go to her in strange and alien St. Louis, to plead his case, to beg her, implore her, to dare ask her if she'd had enough abandoned and filthy sex with her seducer; but feared that she certainly would accept his pleadings, his tears, with perverse delight, would abuse him with a word or two of contempt, and send him home alone. He knew this, knew that she was a bitch, a worthless bitch, shallow and corrupt and cruel: oh how he wanted her, she was *his* bitch! He asked his host then if he would consent to go to St. Louis and, through his friend at the university, meet with his wife, plead for him, set out his case for him, ask her why she'd left, ask her, ask her, *ask* her, even if he had to do it in front of her smirking lover. He would pay for his trip, his airfare and all expenses, and even include a bonus for his trouble, although he was not so totally unbalanced as to use the word "bonus." And so the friend left, but was back within three days, for his wife and her amour had apparently left St. Louis, and there was no way of knowing where they had gone. The husband, in his by-now usual imbecilic daze, finally left his friends' apartment after finding one of his own, a dark and wretched shotgun flat on Fourth Street and Avenue D, a perfect venue to complement his mood of not-quite-suicidal misery. How the streets churned with ignorance and poverty and hatred and violence. Perfect.

The weeks passed and he began, slowly, very slowly, to consider the rash frenzy, really, of his request to his "friend," the weakness he had revealed to him in his unvarnished pleading that he go as his—what was it?—representative? intermediary? envoy? to his wife. He had exposed himself to this man and his wife, and he was certain that he had given them a social or psychological gift that they would use against him in some way in the future, he didn't know when, but at some moment in a year or two or more, he'd be confronted with the whining, puerile, blubbering image of his collapse into bathos, he would be *presented*, as it were, as a milquetoast to whomever would listen. For now it was clear to him that the couple he had thought of with such dismissive contempt for so many years, had thought of him in the same way.

COMMENTARIES

— I —

... *Kraft French Dressing, glowing weirdly orange* ... The label on the bottle describes this dressing as "creamy." So it was in 1934, so it is now. No one has ever discovered why this dressing, with its odd tang of sugary vinegar, was and is called "French," nor has anyone suggested a reason for its strange, pumpkin-like color. It is highly popular.

... *a bottle of Worcestershire sauce* ... This sauce was Lea and Perrins, considered by virtually everyone to be the *ne plus ultra* of Worcestershire sauces. The brand has been made since 1835, and its paper wrapper surely adds to its special cachet. For many years, the label on the bottle noted that it was the recipe of a "nobleman in the county," or, perhaps, "country," but that information is no longer provided.

— II —

. . . the Shadow . . . The Shadow's name was Lamont Cranston, and his assistant and (perhaps) fiancée and/or lover was Margo Lane. She was always described as "the lovely Margo Lane."

. . . Philco floor-model radio . . . Philco radios have not been manufactured for many years.

. . . his black cloak and black slouch hat . . . While the Shadow wore such raiment in the pulp stories conceived by author Walter B. Gibson, producers of the radio version, which concerns us here, working within the constraints of the medium, imbued the character with a secret power that he had "learned in the Orient," the power "to cloud men's minds so that they cannot see him." Nor, of course, could listeners: it could not have mattered what he wore.

. . . his unearthly laughter . . . The Shadow was good, a fighter of crime and oppression, yet the boy is terrified. This might suggest that children know that good may instantly become evil, and vice versa.

— III —

. . . standing at a dark window . . . Fictional characters who stand at dark windows are often constrained to look down at streets gleaming with rain. But not here.

— IV —

. . . his mother sits with a highball . . . In this instance, Canada Dry ginger ale and Seagram's 7 blended whisky. The term "highball" is no longer in general use.

. . . he has been talking, quarreling . . . The quarrel was about money, specifically, a loan from his father-in-law on which the father would like to delay payment. His wife has taken her father's side in this argument, not, perhaps, a good sign for the stability of the marriage.

— V —

. . . a drone of music . . . It may be inferred that the narrator does not like the music in question. But the conversation? What deductive inference are we to draw from the singular selection, for further commentary, of one type of "drone"?

. . . The cab was waiting . . . A checker cab, one of the small, lost pleasures of New York life.

. . . wearing his wife's clothes . . . This is somewhat puzzling. Either the woman was the wife's size, or the wife's clothing was of the one-size-fits-all variety.

— VI —

. . . his wife dead for many years . . . His wife's name was Constance (Connie), and his children's Rose, Maria, Grace, and Alexander (Alex).

— VII —

. . . Carol and . . . the girls' last names, in order, are: Brookner, Kalmas, Margolis, Imperato, Jorgensen, Pincus, Aquino, Griffin, Wasserman, Chaves, Newman, Bello, Scisorek, Vail, and Kirkjian.

. . . the shade of a birch tree . . . It may have been a poplar, or whatever you prefer.

— VIII —

. . . store-brand English muffin . . . The store, A&P; the brand, Jane Parker.

. . . peanut butter . . . The peanut butter is also the A&P's own brand. Ann Page.

. . . a cigarette . . . He smokes Camel Lights and Marlboro Lights.

. . . the old story of the death camp survivor . . . The story: after being liberated from Auschwitz, a Jew tells another Jew that he's going to leave soon for Brazil or Chile or Laos or Pakistan—someplace that is not in Europe. The other Jew says, "It's so *far!*", to which the first Jew replies, "Far from what?"

— IX —

. . . the sliding glass door . . . This suggests, but does not, certainly, prove, that the mise-en-scène is California.

. . . it presented a message . . . E.g., "Hello! You've been selected for a Caribbean vacation!"

. . . he'd had a friend . . . This unexpected event occurred a month or so after the friend had published his first book of poems. There is probably no significance to this, although another "friend" of the poet said that perhaps he's read his own work.

— X —

. . . loves a girl, who, as it turns out . . . The reader may be reminded of the last lines of *Swann's Way* (Moncrieff-Kilmartin translation): "to think that I've wasted years of my life, that I've longed to die, that I've experienced my greatest love, for a woman who didn't appeal to me, who wasn't even my type!" It should be noted, however, that Proust tells us that Swann said this to himself in a period of his "intermittent caddishness."

. . . anything you can dream up . . . You might wish to make on the fly leaves of this book some of the things you can dream up, if you wish; the reader is the ruler.

. . . relentlessly invents its gods . . . It is, of course, distressingly clear that many societies believe that their gods have not been invented but have permitted themselves to be revealed. There were also many extinct societies that believed in revealed gods. The latter are also extinct, despite the occasional romantic attempt to pretend otherwise.

. . . "in mysterious ways" . . . "God works in mysterious ways" is one of the supreme bromides of our age, and this is the age of bromides, many of them disguised as hardheaded observations of life.

— XI —

. . . *the Angelus is heard* . . . The morning Angelus prayer in the Roman Catholic church is announced by the ringing of church bells at 6:00 a.m. In this case, the bells are ringing in the belfry of the Visitation Academy, a school for Catholic girls, in Bay Ridge, Brooklyn.

. . . *in Dr. Denton pajamas* . . . One-piece children's pajamas, often of cotton flannel, their distinguishing feature is the presence of foot coverings, so that the wearer has, so to speak, built-in "slippers" on the garment. They were especially popular in the thirties and forties.

— XII —

. . . *smoking one cigarette after another* . . . In this particular case, Philip Morris cigarettes, the package of which was designed to look like a cured tobacco leaf.

. . . *the husband's Zippo lighter* . . . This lighter had a matte nickel finish.

. . . *a gold graduation-gift fountain pen* . . . This was an Eversharp Skyline fountain pen of 14K gold. Its companion mechanical pencil had been broken for years, and languished in a kitchen drawer.

. . . *She was, of course, pregnant* . . . She may well have been made pregnant by her husband, but he didn't think so.

— XIII —

... *sliced open his gum* ... The dentist—in a case such as this, surely, an oral surgeon—will replace the lost bone with liquid bone (biphasic calcium phosphate, or BCP), which ideally will grow as naturally as the patient's own bones, ultimately replacing it, so that he is "as good as new."

... *and removes her skirt* ... Fantasies of sexual adventures with providers of medical care would seem to be well-nigh universal, at least among male patients.

— XIV —

... *in the best tradition of the deathless cliché* ... "deathless cliché" is, of course, a deathless cliché.

... *still famous for his charming mediocrities* ... That's *your* opinion.

— XV —

... *a sun-faded lime-green monster* ... The term "lime-green" does not truly describe the color of this vehicle, which was of one never seen or even approximated in nature.

... *he took $147.34* ... In 1960, this was a considerable sum. A yearly income of $5,000–$6,000 was enough to live on quite comfortably.

— XVI —

. . . *at the Medical Field Service School* . . . The school was attached to the Brooke Army Medical Center.

. . . *The sky was turning rose and blue* . . . Rimbaud dated "Rêvé pour L'Hiver" October 7, 1870, noting that it was composed "En Wagon," or aboard a train. While it is rarely, if ever, a good idea to attempt a translation—a transliteration—of poetry into prose, this does have some of the flavor of the original—lacking, of course, Rimbaud's brilliant casualness, his arrogant and elegant linguistic slouch.

— XVII —

. . . *smelled of rancid and sour fat* . . . In the early part of the twentieth century, this smell might have been called, in some working-class circles, "a far-away smell."

. . . *the way of Greek warriors* . . . Other Greek warriors who dressed their hair in such wise: Agamemmnon, Menelaus, Ajax (both Great and Lesser), etc., etc.

. . . *Odysseus* . . . Odysseus was red-headed, a sign, perhaps, of his Achean roots.

. . . *"a groove, man!"* . . . Like, excellent. Back-formation, "Groovy."

— XVIII —

. . . *the booth of the diner* . . . It might have been the Royal, Homer's, Kirk's, or the Bridge View.

— XIX —

. . . white rayon underpants . . . In the thirties, these were called "step-ins," a curiously obvious name.

. . . her lunch dishes . . . Dishes probably bought at the local Woolworth five and ten. They were probably decorated with lead-painted flowers, or multicolored stripes.

— XX —

. . . under a mortar attack . . . The expertise of the Chinese with mortars was well-known among American troops during the Korean War.

. . . FECOM . . . An acronym for Far East Command.

— XXI —

. . . an improvisatory fantasia . . . There are many marriages that are based upon "improvisatory fantasias," and why not? The notions of "honesty" in marriage, the revelation of all secrets, and "realism" seem to come from popular fiction of all sorts.

. . . "swell" . . . A word that is no longer in use, save ironically. The late painter and writer, Fielding Dawson, however, used the word without a trace of irony.

— XXII —

. . . a little girl in pigtails . . . These two figures looked vaguely dated.

. . . Handsome is as handsome does . . . This expression may, for some who are not concerned with linguistic subtleties, be transliterated, so to speak, as "actions speak louder than words."

— XXIII —

. . . AMEN DICO VOBIS QUIA UNUS VERSTRUM ME TRADITURUS EST *. . .* Which may be translated: "Amen, I say to you, there is one [of you] who will betray me."

. . . in a summer pinafore . . . The pinafore is pink and white.

. . . The Make-Believe Ballroom . . . a radio program hosted by the D.J. Martin Block. The theme song, "It's Make-Believe Ballroom Time," was, I believe, the Glenn Miller version.

. . . to Jersey City?! . . . Jersey City was, and probably still is, unprepossessing at the best of times; in the "bitter cold" it could be thoroughly dispiriting.

. . . Lux Radio Theater . . . The hallmark of this radio drama series was its presentation, as aural dramas, of the popular movies of the era. Lana Turner may well have starred in the radio version of *The Postman Always Rings Twice*.

. . . Bix Beiderbecke's "Margie" . . . "Margie," a popular song, with words by Benny Davis, music by Con Conrad and J.

Russel Robinson, published in 1920. It was performed, perhaps most famously, by Eddie Cantor in the film, *Margie*. The Beiderbecke performance, here noted, was recorded in New York on September 21, 1928, by Bix Beiderbecke and his Gang. The personnel were: Beiderbecke, cornet, Bill Rank, trombone, Izzy Friedman, clarinet, Min Leibrook, bass saxophone, Roy Bargy, piano, and Lennic Hayton, ordinarily a pianist, on drums. Bix plays with his usual heartbreaking clarity of tone. It's pleasant to think otherwise, but Martin Block would probably never had had Bix's "Margie" on his playlist.

— XXIV —

. . . had he a wife . . . This may suggest that Vince once had a wife but no longer had one, or it may suggest nothing of the kind.

. . . next shopping trip . . . To the A&P or Bohack's.

. . . the favored cereal . . . In this case, Post Toasties, the General Foods Corporation's apparent attempt at whimsy.

— XXV —

. . . sunbaked funereal places . . . E.g.: Las Vegas, NV; Palm Springs, CA; Phoenix, AZ; St. Augustine, FL; Santa Fe, NM; etc.

. . . an accounting ledger . . . Purchased at his local stationery store, Laverty & Son, on Eighth Avenue between Thirteenth and Fourteenth Streets in New York. The store no longer exists.

— XXVI —

. . . canned 3.2 beer from a case . . . The beer, from an Army beer hall, had an alcohol content of 3.2%, and was slightly more potent than water.

. . . the beer hall . . . The beer hall in question was at Fort Hood, Texas; at the time—Spring 1952—THE home of the Second Armored Division ("Hell on Wheels"). No officers were anywhere in sight on this wholly uneventful day.

. . . one had Lone Star, the other Pearl . . . Two brands of beer that were and, taking into account various corporate acquisitions, nominally still are indigenous to Texas.

. . . It was Rosie! . . . "Rosie" was Marvin Rosenthal, a corporal with the Seventh Infantry Division; "Koenig" was Walter Koenig, a PFC from the same division.

. . . chickenshit motherfucker platoon sergeant . . . The reference is to SFC Luther Crittenden, also of the Seventh Division.

— XXVII —

. . . More stories . . . The reader may make his own list, and may be astonished to realize how long it finally is.

. . . Henry James . . . No writer's antennae have ever been as good at detecting well-mannered social and sexual sadism.

— XXVIII —

... its rejection slip clipped ... I have no idea if the *New Yorker* uses or used formal rejection slips.

... printed-out "stuff" ... Steve thought the word "stuff" democratic and non-elite, it perhaps made him feel like Clifford Odets, although in any case the word seems somewhat out of place in connection with electrostatically transferred, heat and pressure-fused printed documents.

... in a writing workshop with Steve at the New School ... "Writing for Publication" was the official title of the course.

— XXIX —

... admitted to the hospital immediately ... The hospital was the Caledonia, located on Prospect Park South. It is now called the Caledonian Campus of the Brooklyn Hospital Center. The nurse's aides wore plaid jumpers.

... he'd drive him in his car ... the car was a 1951 Olds.

... lit one of his Lucky Strikes ... By now, of course, in their wartime white package, the switch from OD being a great advertising coup—profit in patriotism.

— XXX —

... at his wife's office ... The office was the Kew Gardens Branch of Thermo-Fax Sales, a division of 3M.

... a gym or an aerobics class ... Aerobics classes were virtually unknown in the fifties and sixties.

. . . three "really encouraging" letters . . . There were no letters, but he began to believe that he had been praised and
encouraged by various flunkeys working at *Thanatos, Cistern,
Blackfriars Review,* and, amazingly, *The New Cadmean.*

. . . down in the romantic Caribbean . . . Natives usually do
not use the word "romantic" to describe that part of the world.

— XXXI —

. . . days of Juicy Fruit . . . The flavor of this chewing gum has
no relation to any fruit known to man.

. . . and the Milano Restaurant . . . This restaurant persists
in memory as being located on West Fortieth Street near
Eighth Avenue.

. . . existent only in his mother's stories . . . One of which was
that his father had spent $1,000 for a cigar as they left the
Milano: the implication was that this "transaction" was
slightly illegitimate, perhaps even criminal.

. . . drunk on cheap whiskey . . . E.g., Wilson "That's All,"
Paul Jones, Schenley Silver Label, Fleischmann's, Four Roses,
Three Feathers.

. . . whom he always thought of, to be truthful, as a hambone.
. . . Although he was a wonderfully demonic Mr. Hyde, an
erotically charged fiend.

— XXXII —

. . . who lived in the apartment above his . . . Perhaps he had what used to be called a "club foot."

. . . whose wife had died in misery . . . Cause of death unknown.

. . . whose children were callous . . . They were minimally attentive, but cold and distant; this may have had something to do with the fact that they believed he had little or no savings.

. . . lovely of face and figure . . . The phrase is not actually "written," but lies at the side of the road.

. . . did not say what he thought . . . Let's assume that he thought nothing at all.

— XXXIII —

. . . the book of poetry . . . Title: *The Future of Eternity*; the publisher was Knopf. The reviews compared the poems—famously—with those of Elizabeth Bishop, a bad sign.

. . . his street crusted over . . . This was in Bay Ridge, Brooklyn, where Colonial Road "becomes" Marine Avenue.

. . . that he'd never given up smoking . . . It was too late, anyway: he had developed lung cancer which had metastasized to his brain (these are some of the brands of cigarettes he smoked over some sixty years in rough chronological order: Wings, Twenty Grand, Sweet Caporal, Old Gold, Philip Morris, Pall Mall, Herbert Tareyton, Lucky Strikes, Camel, Gauloises, Marlboro Lights, Camel Filters).

— XXXIV —

. . . into the mountains . . . The mountains are easier to imagine than the sea, which almost always confounds memory.

. . . amusement park . . . Cf. Steeplechase, Luna Park, Dreamland.

. . . blew her skirt up . . . This was one of the cruder amusements at Steeplechase in the 1940s.

. . . the Big Lasso . . . This was a ride much like the Whip— rough and unsubtle.

. . . his convertible . . . A 1948 Buick.

. . . real ferryboats once made regular runs . . . The boats were small and painted a curiously drab olive green.

. . . or so Boys' Life *reported . . .* In a piece by Carl Olssen, "Temptation in the Woods."

. . . "My beer is Rheingold, the dry beer" . . . Rheingold beer was brewed in Brooklyn, NY, and was famous for its Miss Subways monthly displays in subways, cars, and buses.

. . . Flagg Brothers . . . These shoes were highly popular among high school boys ca. 1945–1947. They *had* to be dyed cordovan or were considered beneath contempt and unwearable.

— XXXV —

. . . to ride up to her thighs . . . Women always seem to know when they are "showing something," as they say. (This phrase may be obsolete or quaint.)

. . . intentions were very clear . . . Crude behavior often mutely begs forgiveness if presented or enacted as impossible to reign in, "natural."

... roughly, angrily yanked her skirt down ... Eros is to be found everywhere at this party, working, however, rather fitfully.

— XXXVI —

... mediocre state university ... What was called, in saner times, a "rube school" or a "football school."

... Redwood Review ... Its original title was *Eldorado Review,* rather pointedly named after the erstwhile Cadillac model.

— XXXVII —

... King Assembly Agency ... An assembly agency consolidates freight and packs it into freight cars for countrywide destinations. In New York, the working platforms for such labor were in the West Forties near the slaughterhouses.

... this frozen center of his body ... This figure may be considered a metaphor, a metonymy, a synechdoche, or a blunt symbol.

— XXXVIII —

... impressed his teachers ... These teachers knew, in effect, nothing about art, and taught their students from color reproductions of "famous paintings." The course in art appreciation was taught once a week.

. . . Provincetown softball games . . . Some of the players and onlookers became very famous, others simply disappeared or taught at the Art Students League for many years.

. . . he moved to England . . . An excellent way to get him offstage.

— XXXIX —

. . . Talmud, Buddha . . . These are, of course, not religions.

. . . her White Robe . . . The devil, it is said, has many wiles, white robes on well-built women being but one of them. Satan calls this costume "Jerry Falwell's Breakdown."

— XL —

. . . scrub woods and dry grass . . . Of whatever kind. (This passage sounds like a dream, at any rate.)

. . . picturesque seaside town . . . E.g., Carmel, Tiburon, Sausalito: these are not really towns but theme parks representing quaint charm (there used to be a good seafood restaurant in Tiburon).

. . . is performing oral sex . . . This is definitely a dream, or an invented dream—makes little difference.

. . . he begins to cry . . . It's about time to reread "The Interpretation of Dreams": Freud is right even when he's wrong.

— XLI —

... *that performer's weary shtick* ... Which shtick is, astonishingly, admired by many, Crown Heights accent included.

... *Kamenstein's, Forest Green* ... The color was very close to one called North Woods. It somehow *breathed* depression and despair.

— XLII —

... *an orphanage* ... There is no information as to whether or not the orphanage was run by sadists, but given the era, it seems likely.

... *Patton's Third Army* ... The Second Armored Division was Patton's favorite division, called "Hell on Wheels." Its soldiers wore their unit patches on their left pockets, "close to their hearts."

... *the moment he put a brush to canvas* ... Many painters love to tell this story about their early beginnings.

... *blood and agony and horror* ... A good argument can be and has been made for the opinion that everyone killed in war is killed in vain, but it's the dying man's job to point out that we survive in vain.

— XLIII —

... *written by a stranger* ... His best books were *Farsighted*, *Ghost Talk*, *Azure Piano*, and *A Small Hotel*. He couldn't bear to reread any of them.

. . . He wasn't much good for anything else . . . Despite what seemed to be rueful protestations, he didn't *want* to be good for anything else.

. . . doomed to blunder through the shadows of this pervasive twilight . . . This is, admittedly, a melodramatic phrase.

— XLIV —

. . . diet and exercise and meditation . . . As everyone knows, Death is always standing on the corner, sucking on a toothpick and waiting for an assignment.

— XLV —

. . . a touch of the whore . . . A deliberately inflammatory phrase.

. . . he no longer desired his wife . . . This is a not-uncommon state of affairs.

. . . Lawton, Oklahoma . . . Fort Sill had made this grim burg possible.

. . . "the old homestead," as the whole family liked to call it . . . This is not true.

. . . too-tight sweater . . . Satan was happy to reveal her nipples to Dad.

. . . smoking and looking out . . . She was partial to Pall Malls, which one Jack McCarthy called "the whore's cigarette."

. . . slept in bathtubs or in the car . . . And sometimes without a pillow.

. . . If he even knew she'd left . . . This is an exaggeration. Of
course he knew.

— XLVI —

. . . makes us look anew at literature . . . This "anew" look seems
to occur every publishing season—something like the annual
return of the flu.

— XLVII —

. . . one dump after another . . . E.g., Far West Cafe, Bejar
Saloon, Juan's Chili Cellar, Hot Pepper Place. All these places
served Pearl beer, Jax beer, and Carta Blanca beer, with small
bowls of salted green olives on the side.

. . . a hideously figured shirt . . . Sometimes known as a
"Hawaiian" shirt, it was often referred to in the army as an
"AWOL" shirt, and was, fittingly, a magnet for vindictive M.P.'s.

. . . the Cactus Hotel . . . Not a bad name for a Southwestern
fleabag circa 1950.

. . . chaotic Sunday look . . . The barracks looks as if it will
never be clean or orderly again.

. . . hot Meskin ass . . . The speaker might have said "pussy";
in this context, the words are interchangeable.

. . . "Fuckin' A" . . . this expression was supposedly first used
by soldiers of the 1st Army, which patch was a stylized capital
A. The expression implies strong agreement.

— XLVIII —

... *"Eyetalians"* ... Few people, save for clusters of yahoos, pronounce the word this way: a triumph for tolerance.

... *a* faint *accent* ... His accent, like hers, was almost pure New York (see *The Oxford Companion to the English Language*, p.693-4).

... *gray Persian lamb coat* ... A prized fur in the forties and early fifties, thought to be more fashionable and chic than black fur.

... *Black Hand* ... An "American" term for the Mafia or Cosa Nostra: never used by Italians or Sicilians, a kind of tabloid name.

— XLIX —

... *like cultists* ... And/or those who chat with God.

... *smoked a lot of marijuana* ... E.g., Bangalore Blast, Mexicali Mania, Super Head, etc.

... *rebels* ... The word is used with pronounced irony, of course.

... *broccoli-rutabaga casserole* ... This dish may taste better than it sounds.

... *a macramé class* ... An "adult education" class.

... *carrot cake* ... Her secret ingredient was a pinch of thyme.

... *Akina* ... whose real name was Arlene.

... *diligently fake disreputability* ... This was about the time when the Dom closed and the Electric Circus took its place. It was the beginning of the end of the Lower East Side, now a neighborhood of staggeringly, albeit carefully disguised, bourgeois sensibilities.

— L —

. . . didn't understand Los Angeles . . . Los Angeles cannot be understood.

. . . sunny, blue Los Angeles day . . . the sort of day that rapists and mass killers come out to pursue their interests.

. . . performed fellatio . . . No dream: the man wore a filthy Deere cap.

. . . New York was of no help . . . It didn't even *look* as if it could be of help, unlike L.A., which seemed to explode with optimism and gold in the streets.

. . . pull-out Carlyle couch . . . This may well have been a Carlyle copy.

. . . Svengali . . . A lot has been written about Svengali, but few are prepared to believe that he ran a Kosher dairy restaurant in Minsk.

. . . What did St. Louis look like? . . . He imagined a different city each time he thought of the place.

. . . strange and alien St. Louis . . . Well . . . maybe, but pedestrian.

Some of these commentaries may not be wholly reliable.

GILBERT SORRENTINO (1929–2006) is the author of more than thirty books, including the classic *Mulligan Stew* and two novels that were finalists for the PEN/Faulkner Award: *Little Casino* and *Aberration of Starlight*. A luminary of American literature, he was a boyhood friend of Hubert Selby, Jr., a confidant of William Carlos Williams, and the recipient of a Lannan Literary Lifetime Achievement Award. Once an editor at Grove Press, Sorrentino taught at Stanford University for many years before returning to his native Brooklyn.

OTHER COFFEE HOUSE PRESS
BOOKS BY GILBERT SORRENTINO

A STRANGE COMMONPLACE
ISBN 978-1-56689-182-0 | $14.95 | NOVEL

Borrowing its title from a William Carlos Williams poem, *A Strange Commonplace* lays bare the secrets and dreams of characters whose lives are intertwined by coincidence and necessity, possessions and experience.

LUNAR FOLLIES
ISBN 978-1-56689-169-1 | $14 | STORIES

Lunar Follies takes readers on a deliciously absurd voyage through 53 imaginary gallery, museum, and performance art exhibitions in a satirical guidebook perfect for art lovers and the artistically challenged alike.

THE MOON IN ITS FLIGHT
ISBN 978-1-56689-152-3 | $16 | STORIES

Bearing his trademark balance between exquisitely detailed narration, ground-breaking form, and sharp insight into modern life, Gilbert Sorrentino's definitive collection of stories spans 35 years of his writing career and contains previously unpublished work and stories that first appeared in *Harper's*, *Esquire*, and *The Best American Short Stories*.

LITTLE CASINO
ISBN 978-1-56689-126-4 | $14.95 | NOVEL

In this superb novel composed of fragments of memory, Gilbert Sorrentino captures the unconventional nuances of a conventional world amidst the grit of golden-era Brooklyn. In episodes affectingly textured with penetrating detail, Sorrentino ferrets out the gristle and beauty found in the voices of the scrappy immigrant boys, hard drinking men, and poor, sexy, magenta-lipped women who inhabit the novel.

COLOPHON

The Abyss of Human Illusion was designed at Coffee House Press, in the historic
Grain Belt Brewery's Bottling House near downtown Minneapolis.
The text is set in Caslon.

FUNDER ACKNOWLEDGMENTS

Coffee House Press receives major operating support from the Bush Foundation, the
McKnight Foundation, from Target, and from the Minnesota State Arts Board, through an
appropriation by the Minnesota State Legislature and from the National Endowment for the
Arts. We have received project support from the National Endowment for the Arts, a federal
agency; the Jerome Foundation; and the National Poetry Series. Coffee House also receives
support from: three anonymous donors; Abraham Associates; the Elmer L. and Eleanor J.
Andersen Foundation; Allan Appel; Around Town Literary Media Guides; Bill Berkson; the
James L. and Nancy J. Bildner Foundation; the Patrick and Aimee Butler Family Foundation;
the Buuck Family Foundation; Dorsey & Whitney, LLP; Fredrikson & Byron, P.A.; Jennifer
Haugh; Anselm Hollo and Jane Dalrymple-Hollo; Jeffrey Hom; Stephen and Isabel Keating;
Robert and Margaret Kinney; the Kenneth Koch Literary Estate; Allan & Cinda Kornblum;
Seymour Kornblum and Gerry Lauter; the Lenfestey Family Foundation; Ethan J. Litman;
Mary McDermid; Rebecca Rand; Debby Reynolds; Schwegman, Lundberg, Woessner, P.A.;
Charles Steffey and Suzannah Martin; John Sjoberg; Jeffrey Sugerman; Stu Wilson and Mel
Barker; the Archie D. & Bertha H. Walker Foundation; the Woessner Freeman Family
Foundation in memory of David Hilton; and many other generous individual donors.

NATIONAL
ENDOWMENT
FOR THE ARTS

*This activity is made possible
in part by a grant from the
Minnesota State Arts Board,
through an appropriation by the
Minnesota State Legislature
and a grant from the National
Endowment for the Arts.* MINNESOTA
STATE ARTS BOARD

TARGET.

To you and our many readers across the country,
we send our thanks for your continuing support.

Good books are brewing at www.coffeehousepress.org